For Edith with
much Love, Joanne

The Country of My Room

Also by Joanne Saltzman

The Back Dock and other poems

The Country of My Room

◆◆◆

by

Joanne Saltzman

ISBN: 9798667112914 (paperback)

For my grandfather, Louis Fried, with everlasting gratitude
For my husband, Alan, with everlasting love

Contents

Part I

Memoir (1982–2020)

The Country of My Room

I spent my first eight years living with my mother and father in New York City on the Upper West Side. We lived on the eleventh floor. Our apartment's front door was painted black, with a gold plate and shiny black numbers on it: 1101. Today I would probably find the apartment small, but then the four-room dwelling seemed massive and explore worthy.

Upon entering our apartment, if I walked straight through the foyer, I'd get to my room. If instead, I made a left, I'd be in the living room pretty quickly. From the living room, I could get to my parents' bedroom. It was a continent unto itself and my most desired destination. I longed to be in that room whenever I was home. It smelled like my parents whether they were in it or not.

I wanted to sleep in their bed, and many nights I would leave my bed, travel through the foyer into the living room, and arrive at their closed door. I'd open it, tiptoe in, and climb from the foot end up the middle and get under the covers between them. In the morning, my dad would be happy to see me, and my mom would not. She didn't mind my being in their room any other time, just not when they slept. Even with her stern warnings about getting a lock (which she never did), I couldn't stop going into their room many nights during their marriage.

My room was a country made up of many places. My bed was on the right-hand wall. Being on my bed was being in one of the places. If I lay facing the wall, I felt contained and safe. If I faced into the room, my eyes came to rest on the huge oil painting hung on the left-hand wall. It was of my mother and her sister, Cynthia, as children seated on a bench in a pastoral setting. She was about eight, and her sister was about four. My mom had a mature expression on her face, as if life had already gotten to her. She looked like she had trudged obligingly to the bench because she had to, because everything she did was because she had to. The painting scared me, and I would ask my mom to remove it, but she said it was just she and my aunt as children and I shouldn't be scared of it, and her tone told me the discussion was over.

I spent a lot of time sitting on the green linoleum floor playing with my dolls or moving my wooden trains on their tracks. I loved being on the floor. It was the central place of my room; it went everywhere I could see. I'd organize my dolls into families. The babies got the most attention because they were little and cute. The older sisters were jealous of the babies, but too bad. The mommy was bossy but could be understanding. The daddy was at work. I spoke for my dolls like dialogue in a play. I believed they were alive while I did it. They kept me company.

All my toys and dolls were for me. I had no siblings to talk to or fight with about our stuff. When I had a friend over, I gave her whatever she wanted to play with; I was so glad to have her there.

Another place in my room was my closet. Entering it, I was transported. When I closed the door, it surrounded me like a womb. I didn't do much in it, just sat looking at my neatly hung clothing and purposely placed shoes. It was quiet in my room, but it was silent in my closet. I could hear my breathing.

I always woke up early, before my parents. I had to amuse myself quietly until they awoke and I could put on the television. I would leave my room excitedly, bound for the vast playground of the living room. The sun was there ahead of me, lighting and warming the sofa and stuffed chairs that held their positions faithfully. My first stop was a red high-back armchair. I'd climb onto the left arm and straddle it, holding on to the arm's wing, riding my horsey. Next, I'd go to another armchair and ride that horsey. When I was done riding, I'd stand up on the couch facing the mirror that hung over it and study my teeth, wiggling any loose ones. I couldn't wait to lose a tooth and have a visit from the tooth fairy. She wasn't Santa Claus by any stretch, but still.

For eight years in apartment 1101, my mother, father, and I looked like the family in the stories read to me. I was the baby bear in the Goldilocks story, and I had a mama and papa. Goldilocks sits in each chair, but only the baby bear's chair feels "just right." I knew I was a little girl like Goldilocks, not really a bear, and I wanted to feel "just right." I wanted my mother and father to feel that way too. I needed to believe that we fit together like the family of bears.

My parents had married quickly, my father fresh from fighting overseas in World War II and my mother practically a spinster in those days, still single at twenty-three. Just two months after their hasty yet extravagant wedding in 1946, my mother unexpectedly found herself expecting me. She and my father were living in a hotel. They had not even found an apartment yet. They grabbed apartment 1101 and set it up shortly before my birth. They were still relative strangers to each other, reeling from their impulsive decision to marry.

What "fit" was apartment 1101 and its contents. It was the firm and fertile soil I needed to grow. I could open myself in its light as I moved from room to room, secure that each place would be there when I entered and remain there in absence. The same could not always be said of my parents. My father's tension toward my mother, his impatience with her, made my stomach hurt. My mother's failed attempts to connect with my father became my fault somehow in my spongy absorption of their troubled marriage.

Still, our appearance as the family who lived in apartment 1101 sustained me. Like my fairy tales where everyone lived happily ever after, I was doing that, too, stomachache and all.

After eight years, we moved to another apartment some fifteen blocks away. My mother took me there while it was someone else's home, with their stuff in it. We walked through the rooms, including the one my mother said would be mine. It was a surreal walk that had nothing to do with me, with where I lived.

Shortly after, I found myself on that foreign terrain again. My mother had hired a decorator and started over. None of the furniture from apartment 1101 survived. She didn't even want the portrait of her and my aunt. I had a brand-new bed that rested on the newly laid carpet alongside all the other alien items that had been preselected for me without my awareness or opinion. The country of my room had been destroyed, erased from its spot in the world.

Less than a year after the move, my parents divorced. There, amid the coordinated colors of chrome-themed furnishings, my father packed his belongings and started for the door.

That was in 1956, shortly after my ninth birthday. Almost fifty years later, my father suffered a stroke. By then, he lived in California, while I lived in New York City. He and I spoke on the phone about once a month but had not seen each other for a number of years. While not estranged, we lived mainly separate lives.

I immediately flew to California, where he was hospitalized and thankfully stable. Despite the awkward emotional distance between us, my father told me that it still haunted him how on the day he moved out, I grabbed onto his legs at the door and begged him not to leave. He had never mentioned this before. I had no recollection of that actual day, no memory of doing what he said I did. I stared numbly at his ancient head on the pillow and tried to picture myself as that child of nine, prone on the floor, pulling at his suit pants, maybe even gripping the muscles of his legs. It was hard to imagine myself pleading for him to stay, my need so raw, so exposed. I had nostalgic, well-preserved memories of my creative, solitary survival on my terra firma in apartment 1101. I had only remembered grieving the loss of that first apartment, of my room—a grief I experienced over and over again into adulthood whenever I had to finally get rid of a broken-down piece of furniture or, worse, when I had to move from one residence to the next. I held on to items way past their use or need because to lose them felt so painfully irrevocable.

I looked at my father as he began to doze off. He had no idea that his words had started a tear in the fabric of my identity. I hardly realized myself that day, but as the months following it became years, I found that I was no longer a woman who couldn't handle letting go of her couch, her old clothes, even her home.

Those things were replaceable, unlike the family I had lost when my father left.

Grandpa Herman Butterman

My father's father was Herman Butterman. My father was his only child, and I was his only grandchild. Grandpa Herman was a treasure of a man. He was devoted to his wife, son, and granddaughter. My first memory of him is when I was five years old, and he and I alone took a walk around the Central Park Reservoir. I held his hand and asked one question after the next. He answered as if his words were white bone china that had to reach my ears delicately and in one piece. When he and my grandmother came to visit us, he would lie down on the living room couch for a rest and spread his white handkerchief under his head. When I asked him why he did it, he said he didn't want to "soil" the couch. I was intrigued by this word and wanted to know what it meant. He explained this and anything else I wanted to know. In fact, if he heard me asking anyone a question, he would write me a long letter explaining the answer. Once he heard me asking my mother how the sky got colored blue. A few days later, I got a beautifully explicit letter from him with the scientific explanation.

My grandfather was an immigrant from Latvia. He and his family came to America on a boat when he was about twelve. He told me that when he got off the boat, someone handed him a banana. For him, it was an exotic fruit, his first banana in the new world. He promptly ate the entire thing, skin and all!

He loved trains and worked as a young man for the railroad in some way, but I don't know more than that, and, sadly, there is no one now to ask. He met my grandmother Sara in New York City, where they both lived in the Bronx. It turned out that she, too, was Latvian and that they were very distantly related. They married on February 11, 1919. My father was born in February of 1921.

My grandfather by then was working on Wall Street. He loved the stock market and worked for the Bache family. When the market crashed in 1929, my grandfather lost all of the money he had made, approximately $60,000, and a fortune for him. He was only in his thirties but suffered a breakdown and a bleeding ulcer. My father recalled that for six months his father was gone from the home. My father was only eight at the time, and no one told him what had happened or where his father was. When my grandfather returned home, he went back to Wall Street and worked again for the Bache family but was never able to accumulate the kind of wealth he had had. Still, he was thankful to be making a good living, and he and my grandmother had a nice apartment on East Thirty-Fifth Street and Lexington Avenue. They enjoyed classical concerts and good restaurants in the city and traveled to Europe for vacations.

Grandpa Herman loved learning. Everything interested him, and he was mainly self-taught. He spoke French, played the violin wonderfully, and had a boundless vocabulary. I got an allowance from him every Sunday. It was a dollar and fifty cents, but I had to earn it. Before he gave me the money, I had to pay attention to a sheet of paper he had with new words or phrases for me to learn. That was the deal. Sometimes he'd have a term like *per capita*, and he'd explain to me what it meant and how it came from when cattle head was counted. He made me eliminate *cannot* from the dictionary. He said it did not exist. His passion for knowledge was contagious and incurable.

He worried a lot about my dad, my grandma, and me. He called me daily, and when I answered the phone, he'd say, "Joanne, darling, are you all right?" as if he'd just heard I'd been in an accident. After his family and knowledge, he loved the violin. He played it by himself at home after dinner. He'd take his glasses off, and he looked so different to me without them. His brown eyes were set deeply in dark-blue sockets. They were curious and sweet, like a child's. The moment he started bowing his violin, his eyes closed shut, as his whole being emitted the sounds the strings made.

He took me to see violinists like Yehudi Menuhin and Zino Francescatti before I had turned ten. At the time, it seemed like a grown-up, boring thing to do, but he was so excited to be taking me that I enjoyed it then and have a lifelong love of classical music as a result. He also took me to my first opera, *Carmen* with Rise Stevens. About ten minutes before the end of it, he insisted that we leave, pulling me up the aisle to get out ahead of the "dying scene," of which he wanted to spare me.

My grandfather was bald by the time I was born. Grandma Sara said he'd had thick red hair when he was younger, and they called him "Rusty." I think maybe that's where I got my auburn hair color. After my parents divorced when I was nine, my dad and I would spend Sundays together and have an early dinner with Grandpa Herman and Grandma Sara. It was there that my grandfather would take me aside, always a special time for just the two of us on his living room couch. He'd take out his sheet of information to teach me before giving me my allowance. He'd hold the paper so carefully and talk meaningfully to me with a purpose I could feel but not truly understand then as I have come to. Imparting to me what he had uncovered in his research was utterly crucial to him. I listened not because of the money, which, while it was nice, was not a huge deal for me, given that money seemed to pour pretty freely around me like water. I just loved how much he wanted to be talking to me, how special I was to him. To matter like that to another human being is the nectar of life. There is no other ingredient like it, and there is no replacement for it.

When I started writing poems as a teenager, he typed each one up with carbon paper so that there were several copies. He was beyond enthusiastic about my poems, even sending them to someone he knew at *The New Yorker* magazine, which was completely unrealistic but nevertheless gave me incredible support.

My grandfather died in March of 1974, when I was twenty-six and living in Los Angeles. He had fallen on an icy street on his way to the subway, still going to Wall Street to work in his eighties. The fall somehow messed with his head and resulted in his having dementia-like symptoms. At that time I was not in the best place in my own life and so had been less in touch with him, plus I was three thousand miles away. Still, I managed to fly to the city and see him at St. Vincent's Hospital. I entered the room, a semiprivate one, and went to his bedside. He seemed disoriented, and his speech was of a babbling and incoherent nature. I hoped he recognized me, but I cannot say for sure that he did. About a week later, he passed away. I am so very grateful I was able to see him that last time.

Grandpa Herman was Jewish but not at all religious. There was no funeral for him, and he was cremated, so he is not buried anywhere I can visit. Over these past forty-five years since he died, I have at times felt his spirit with me, guiding me. Recently, he came to visit me in a dream, and I told him how much I missed him and that I'd written a poem for him. Even when I am not thinking about him, his love and influence are flowing inside the marrow of my bones.

Grandma Sara Butterman

My grandma Sara Butterman had one child, my father, Edward. She married my grandfather, Herman, on February 11, 1919, and gave birth to Edward on February 23, 1921. My grandparents were both from Latvia and were distantly related. I wish I knew how they met and fell in love, but I do not. I think my grandmother was born in New York City, but she may have been born in Latvia like Grandpa Herman and then come over by ship like he had.

When first married, they lived in the Bronx on the Grand Concourse. That's where my father grew up. By the time (1947) that I was born, they lived in New York City, on Thirty-Fifth Street and Lexington Avenue. I spent countless hours at their one-bedroom apartment and loved being there. The entry was raised, and the living room was a few steps down; *sunken* is the real estate term. At the far end of the living room, a few steps led up to the dining area. The two sets of steps with wrought iron handrails were my endless areas of play. I would jump down, clearing all steps from either the foyer or the dining areas, while my grandmother begged me to be careful. I would jump up to those areas as well, again with her concerned warnings.

In their bedroom, they had a picture of me on their dresser. I was about four years old and in a ballet costume posing on a bench, clearly a professional photo.

The other photo on the dresser was of Grandma Sara as a young woman with dark, wavy hair. I would look at it, hardly believing it was she. She was old and had short white hair from the time I was born. Other than the dresser, their room contained a double bed, small night tables, and a little chair. There was not much to do in their room other than sleep. When I spent the night at their apartment, my grandfather would sleep in the living room on a convertible couch, and I would sleep in the double bed next to my grandma. Before falling asleep, we would talk about lots of things. We would lie on our backs, talking into the darkness as if nothing else existed right at that moment, and nothing else did. My questions got answered lovingly and patiently. I must have asked what growing up would be like because I can remember Grandma Sara's voice in the dark telling me that someday I would go out with chaps, and then maybe one of them would end up being my husband. I thought the word *chaps* was much more intriguing than if she'd said I would go out with boys. As we lay there having our talks, I could feel my grandmother loving every second. After raising a son, she was thrilled to have a granddaughter.

My grandmother told me that when she was a little girl, her family was very poor and could not buy her a doll. She said she would stand in front of the toy store window and look longingly at the dolls. She utterly delighted in giving me dolls, which we would then play with. I remember her bringing me a Tiny Tears doll when I was about five or six. She (Tiny Tears) had curly brown hair like mine and came with a bottle and diaper. You could put water in her bottle and feed her through a little hole she had between her lips, and then she'd wet her diaper at the other end! Grandma Sara and I had a lot of fun with her.

I loved comic books, especially *Little Lulu* and *Tubby* ones, and Grandma Sara would read them to me, and we'd laugh out loud. One of the other characters in the *Lulu* comics was Hazel the Witch, and she had a little girl who was called Little Itch.

One day Grandma Sara was reading to me from the comic book, and Hazel and Little Itch were both laughing about something. The bubble above their heads to tell you that said "cackle, cackle" for Hazel and "kickle, kickle" for Little Itch. We laughed so hard reading that—I can still hear us doing so!

In our first apartment, where I lived until I was eight, we only had one telephone located in my parents' bedroom. When I was five or so, I wanted to call Grandma Sara, and my mother told me her phone number—MU5-6905. I said the number over and over until I'd memorized it. The MU stood for Murray Hill, which was the area of the city where my grandmother lived. I spent that afternoon calling Grandma Sara, talking a bit, hanging up, and then calling her right back! I felt utterly empowered by this at the time. I could reach her, hear her voice because I knew her phone number! Finally, I was told "enough," but I still remember that day and how thrilled I was to affect something on my own for the first time.

After my parents divorced, when I was nine, I spent Sundays with my father. We would arrive at Grandma Sara's home in the afternoon, and she would be preparing our dinner. She was a wonderful, wholesome cook, and I loved her meals.

She made simple but delicious meatloaf that was always mouth-wateringly moist.

She baked chocolate brownies from scratch for me without nuts because I didn't like nuts in them. She would wrap extra brownies in wax paper for me to take home.

I always keep wax paper in the kitchen, and when I use it, I think so strongly of her.

In 1969, when, at twenty-two, I became pregnant, my grandma Sara was absolutely ecstatic. She glowed more than I did. We would meet for one of our lunches at Schrafft's on Madison Avenue in the sixties, and afterward we would take a walk, but she didn't want me to exert myself too much and would hail a cab and send me home after we'd walked a bit. When I gave birth, she came to the hospital with a bakery box of heart-shaped cinnamon sugar cookies that were the best I've ever tasted. She said they were her favorites, from a special bakery she loved.

Grandpa Herman passed away in 1974, and my grandmother was devastated.

At the time, I sadly could not properly support her in her grief. I was three thousand miles away, living in Los Angeles, and engulfed in a difficult period in my own life.

Grandma Sara passed away in 1982. For the last several years of her life, she suffered from dementia. In 1981, I came in from LA and visited her at her home, where she lived with round-the-clock nursing care. I felt she recognized me but could not say for sure. She was no longer speaking. Her eyes did seem to alight looking at me. I brought her a Madame Alexander doll, which she seemed to like. I have a picture of her in a chair with the doll next to her on a table. Her eyes are sweet and untroubled. Perhaps the dementia was a blessing for her after losing her beloved husband of fifty-five years. My father paid for her care, saying at the time that his mother would only be put in a facility "over my dead body."

Years later, my father had serious financial problems, but I know for a fact that he never, ever regretted spending the money he had caring for his mother until the end of her life. He was just glad he had the money at that point in time and so was able to keep her in her home.

I was thirty-five when Grandma Sara passed away, on December 16, 1982.

I had the incredible good fortune of having all four grandparents love me and help raise me since we all lived close to each other in the city. I reached the age of twenty-one before losing any of them. I was two days shy of turning forty-one when Grandpa Lou Fried, my last living grandparent, died at ninety-four. Their generous, nurturing love is the foundation of my being.

Author's Note

Like Grandpa Herman, Grandma Sara was cremated. There was no funeral; I just got a phone call from my father that she had passed away.

Still, I wrote "Monologue for Sara" to honor her and to at least imagine going to New York to her funeral.

Monologue for Sara

I will not look out the window. I have pulled down the tight little shade.

Flying has been a huge fear since I was eleven. Now I am thirty-five. Takeoff was deafening, and I shook with terror for twenty minutes until all the signs went off and the captain made his reassuring broadcast over the PA. By then, I was drinking the gin and tonic I had urged the stewardess to bring me "immediately."

This L1011 is cruising at a nervy thirty-eight thousand feet, and I am on gin and tonic number two. But Lord knows you are worth this, and so much more.

Dad said not to come; it wasn't absolutely necessary, considering the distance and money involved. Dad is your only child, and maybe he knows. I am your only granddaughter, your only grandchild, and what I know is that my eternal love for you has put me right here, right now.

I close my eyes, head swirling a bit from the altitude and the gin. I see you as last I did, an eighty-seven-pound withered body assembled on a stuffed chair, a body not consumed with illness but with antiquity, a body that had aged rapidly since losing your husband after fifty-five years of marriage. Dad said it was hard for him to see you that way, your needs once again those of the infant, a nurse tending to them round the clock. For me it was different. I found myself drenched with gratitude for the innocence you had regained, for the absence of your suffering.

I blink and see you with my childhood eyes. My compact, dainty Grandma Sara, smelling like perfume and powder, the woman who gave me doll after pretty doll, as many as she had longed for when herself a child whose parents had no money for such toys. I hear your patient voice reading me stories and comic books. I remember the countless nights when we sent Grandpa Herman to sleep in the living room so you and I could lie snuggled in the dark, talking endlessly. I have so much to remember, even though I feel cheated now of so much more we could have shared. There are so many questions I never got to ask you. So much of our time together I took for granted then and cherish now.

The captain is announcing the start of our descent. Not too much longer, Grandma, and I will be with you once more, to say the Kaddish prayer for you and to say goodbye.

Grandpa Louis Fried

My grandfather Lou Fried was my mother's father. He was a short, stocky man with a blustery face that was always a tad red. He was of Hungarian descent, I believe. What I do know is that he, his parents, and sister were Jewish immigrants who lived on the Lower East Side of Manhattan at the turn of the last century. My grandfather was born on September 14, 1894. When he was ten years old, his father died. I don't know how he died, but it was somewhat sudden because Lou's mother sat him down and told him, "You're the man of the family now. You have to quit school and get a job and take care of your sister and me." Lou was in the fifth grade.

He found a job working for another Jewish immigrant named Joseph Siegel. Joseph had come over from Minsk, Russia, with his parents as a young boy of about twelve.

They had dressed Joseph up as a girl and said he was a daughter so that they could bring him because young boys mattered in Minsk and he would probably have been detained from leaving.

Joseph had a small shoe store on the Lower East Side and hired the young Lou to mind the store, help customers, and run errands. Lou was a hard and earnest worker. He had no time for the luxury of grieving the loss of his father. He couldn't even think about the fact that he had to leave school. It was about survival for Lou, and he had a good job he intended to keep. When winter came, Lou told his mother, "Ma, if it's snowing out, wake me up an hour earlier." When she did this, Lou got to work an hour ahead of schedule. By the time Joseph arrived, Lou (as he loved to tell me) would have "turned over" a lot of business selling galoshes!

Lou and Joseph became close. Lou was in need of a father figure, and Joseph was only too happy to mentor this employee who was so capable and trustworthy.

Joseph had a wife, Sarah, and a three-year-old daughter, Goldie, when Lou first started to work with him. In the years that followed, Joseph and Sarah had three sons—Mac, Irving, and Fred, who arrived in 1910. Lou, so close to the Siegel family by then, was sent to fetch the midwife for Fred's birth!

Joseph and Lou expanded over the years from the one shoe store to getting into the shoe auctioning business and then eventually founding their own company, which they called National Shoes. In the 1950s, when I was a small child, the company had already been a huge success for several years, with a pretty popular ad jingle ("National Shoes, ring the bell") that lots of people knew how to sing.

In 1917, Lou was on some kind of reserve with the US Navy but was not sent overseas to fight in the First World War as far as I know.

In January of 1918, Joseph Siegel's daughter, Goldie, was sixteen and graduating high school. As was the custom at that time, Goldie had a beautiful leather autograph book for her friends to sign for her to keep as a momentum of their time together.

I have that autograph book, which I cherish. It came to me in 1987 when Grandpa Lou asked me, my mother, and Aunt Cynthia to go through the items in his home in New York and take what we wanted before he sold the apartment.

What a treasure to find this book filled with the many pages of Goldie's classmates' best wishes for her. As I turned each page and enjoyed each message, I was surprised to suddenly be reading the words that the twenty-three-year-old Lou had written in Goldie's book:

> To Goldie,
> I wish you that, which you would wish a good friend to wish you for your future success.
>
> Your friend,
> Louis Fried
> Jan. 19, 1918

By 1921, twenty-seven-year-old Lou had fallen in love with twenty-year-old Goldie, and she with him. He had known her since she was a small child, and she had blossomed into a lovely young woman. The irony, as other family members have told me, was that at the time, Sarah, my great-grandmother and Goldie's mother, was not thrilled that Lou had his eye on her daughter. Even though he was such a close family friend, as well as Joseph's business partner, Sarah had higher hopes for her only girl.

Lou had never gone beyond the fifth grade, whereas Goldie had graduated from high school. Sarah thought a doctor, a lawyer, or even a dentist was a more suitable match. Sarah's view was that she and Joseph were immigrants to America; he'd started a business and been financially successful precisely so that his children could have more, take a step up from their parents.

I don't know how Joseph felt about the match, but I have to believe he was much more accepting of it than his wife. Firstly, Lou was like a fourth son to him by the time Goldie was grown. In fact, Joseph was the president of National Shoes and Lou was next in command, and only after him came Joseph's sons as they grew up and joined the family business.

On May 30, 1922, Goldie and Lou were married in New York City. Nine months later, on February 21, 1923, my mother, Lucille, was born. Four years later, Goldie and Lou had a second daughter, my aunt Cynthia, born May 10, 1927.

When my mother was eight months pregnant with me, in September of 1947, Joseph Siegel passed away. By then, he had retired, and Grandpa Lou was president of the company. As my grandfather used to proudly state to me and others, "I never finished fifth grade, but I'm in *Who's Who in America*!"

I was born October 5, 1947, the first grandchild of Goldie and Lou Fried. I was named Joanne after my great-grandfather, Joseph.

Given his most humble beginnings on the Lower East Side of New York City and leaving school in the fifth grade to support his family financially, my grandpa Louis Fried's accomplishments were monumental. National Shoe Company was a nationwide shoe chain of stores that sold popularly priced shoes, socks, and stockings. By the time Lou and Goldie were young parents raising two daughters, they had moved from the Bronx to West End Avenue in Manhattan, about the most affluent residential street at that time.

In the 1950s, Goldie talked Lou into buying a cooperative apartment at Sixty-Seventh Street and Fifth Avenue overlooking Central Park. The building was a "white glove" one, with doormen and elevator attendants. Goldie and Lou had a full-time housekeeper, a Cadillac car, and a full-time chauffeur to drive it. They belonged to a private country club in Westchester and the Palm Beach Country Club in Palm Beach, Florida, where they wintered.

When his wife wanted him to learn how to dance, Grandpa Lou went with her to an Arthur Murray studio and learned the cha-cha, rumba, tango, meringue, and more. He and Goldie dazzled on the dance floor at the black-tie charity affairs they attended in the city and Palm Beach. They traveled a lot and enjoyed seeing the world. Even though it was considered bold to buy one's apartment instead of renting at the time, the beautiful apartment on Fifth Avenue was not only the home they would share for the rest of their lives together, but when Grandpa Lou sold it in 1987, he made over fifty times what he had paid for it.

According to my cousin Ken Siegel, Grandpa Lou was a Freemason, and Ken went with his uncle Lou to Freemason meetings. That is all Ken would divulge about this since it is a secret society of people. I never discussed it with my grandfather while he was living. Lou also embraced *The Science of the Mind* and *The Power of Positive Thinking* to guide him in his later years. He and Goldie were members of Temple Emanu-El in New York City and as a child, I went with them to High Holidays services.

From the time he was ten years old and became the "man of the family," my Grandpa Lou never, ever blinked on that responsibility. He spent his life making sure that his loved ones always had what they needed materially; a home, food on the table, financial security. He showed his love for, and devotion to his family members in this way. He was a practical, no-nonsense kind of man who would not spend his time on a certain type of emotional indulgence – the type that could take his eye off the ball of his responsibility for his wife, daughters, granddaughters and great-grandchildren. That was not going to happen, not on his watch.

Grandpa Louis Fried passed away comfortably at ninety-four years old in 1988.

Grandma Goldie Fried

My maternal grandmother was Goldie Fried. I was very close with her for the twenty-one years, eleven months, and fifteen days that I had her in my life.

I was her first grandchild, and she called me "cookala." When she spoke my name, I felt special, something about how she pronounced it, with the emphasis on the "Jo" part, warmed me every time. Eventually, she had two more granddaughters, my first cousins, Nancy and Wendy, my aunt Cynthia's children, but I lived in the city like Grandma Goldie and spent more time with her. They lived in Westchester.

I was also five years older than Nancy and eight years older than Wendy and so had those years with our grandmother before they were born.

Grandma Goldie was the first child for Sarah and Joseph Siegel. She was born on June 16, 1901, and lived in the Bronx. Sarah went on to have three more babies, each a boy. By the third son, Fred, Goldie had had it! She'd wanted a sister each time, and when she heard it was another brother, she said, "Oh no, another bum!"

In 1922, Goldie married Lou Fried, a dear family friend and business partner of her father's. In 1937, Goldie's youngest brother, Fred, married a beautiful lady named Joan. Goldie and Joan adored each other. While Fred was overseas in World War II, Joan had to undergo massive back surgery and then stay immobile in bed for several months while she healed. In her letters to Fred, she never told him about her situation so as not to upset him. Goldie would come to visit Joan and tell her about the activities she and Lou had done that week, like theater and dinner parties. Then Joan would write to Fred that she had done these things, using Goldie's descriptive information. Fred only found out the truth after he'd made it home from the war.

Goldie and Lou had two daughters, Lucille and Cynthia. They were very different from each other, and each daughter had an intense relationship with her mother.

Lucille was my mom, and she and her mother were not all that close because Goldie had expectations my mother could not meet. My mother was an artsy, intellectual young girl who loved jazz and T. S. Elliott, and my grandma Goldie wanted her daughter to marry well and keep a lovely home.

Cynthia was the second daughter, and she, too, was brainy. When she decided to go to graduate school, eventually getting a PhD in the 1940s, Goldie was worried that no man would want to marry a girl who had more degrees than he did!

Cynthia did marry, but she and her husband did not make it as a couple, and as that marriage began to fail, Cynthia was diagnosed with colitis. She was thirty-six. She spent six months in the hospital, Goldie with her every day. When Cynthia finally recovered, Goldie and Lou helped set her up in an apartment with her two daughters. They had already set up my mother and me in an apartment when my parents divorced. I can only imagine the pain my grandmother felt seeing both her daughters' marriages fail. It was the 1950s when my parents divorced, and that was rare. Maybe it was another reason Goldie stayed so close to me and watched over me so fiercely. My father said he always respected the way Goldie was like a lioness with her cubs.

Grandma Goldie loved to play the piano, and I danced around the living room of her home or mine when she did. She had the key to our apartment after my dad moved out when I was nine, and sometimes I would come home from school to find her playing piano, waiting for me and my mom. She smoked and had a rich, gravelly voice. She had elegant clothes and jewelry, but she was not an accumulator of things. She said she'd rather have a few really special dresses to wear over and over again to the affairs she and Grandpa Lou attended than to keep buying more.

My mom took a cruise to Europe after her divorce, to be a single lady out in the world. I stayed with Grandma Goldie and Grandpa Lou, and it was very soothing. I pretended that they were my parents and that I lived with a happy, devoted couple that doted on me.

Grandma Goldie liked to play Beethoven and Chopin the most. My favorite to dance to was the Chopin "Minute" Waltz. The piece that meant the most to her was Beethoven's eighth piano sonata, the *Pathétique*. She worked at it for most of her life.

When she played it, she melded with the piano. She seemed in a trance until the last note was played. Then, she'd look up, her eyes moist, and she'd give a slight *Mona Lisa* smile.

When her hands became arthritic, she got scared that she wouldn't be able to play the sonata anymore. It was the 1950s, when music was only on records and no one had tape recorders. Grandma Goldie took herself to a studio and had herself recorded playing the *Pathétique*. All these years since she died of a brain tumor in 1969, I still have that record.

We didn't know at first that she had a brain tumor. She'd gotten quiet and glum, and so we thought she was depressed. Grandpa Lou took her to see a psychiatrist, who put her on some mild stimulants, but she didn't respond to them. Meanwhile, her lady friends started complaining that she couldn't keep up with their card or mah-jongg games. Eventually they stopped inviting her to play. Then, at a cocktail party, she stacked chocolate and cheese together on a cracker, and my grandfather realized something was seriously wrong. When he put her in the hospital for tests, she said, "This hotel is lovely!"

I was in my senior year of college at the time and already married. I went from class to the hospital the day she had exploratory surgery. When I went to see her in recovery, she had a shower cap on her head and an angelic expression on her face, like a just-nursed baby. The doctor came into the waiting room and told us her tumor was inoperable and that she had about nine months to live. My grandfather started to cry, the only time I ever had or would see him do that.

I spent the next nine months feeling stunned during the day and crying myself to sleep at night, my face flush into my pillow so my husband wouldn't hear me.

I had never experienced someone close to me dying or even someone I actually knew dying and did not know how to talk to anyone about it, not even him.

I visited my grandma almost daily after class and on the weekends. I would sit and do my homework, looking up at her from time to time or going over to hold her hand. I wanted to be as physically near her body mass as I could. She didn't seem to know me or anything the way she had. She never talked but smiled childlike, and her eyes had a contented gaze that made me utterly grateful for her lack of knowledge or suffering about her illness. She remained in her own sweet state until she went into a coma for the last few weeks and died. I stayed close to her until then. My eyes needed to relish every second spent looking at her, knowing the time would come when they would be denied even that. It was all I could do.

For most of her illness, my grandmother was in her home, an apartment on Sixty-Seventh Street and Fifth Avenue in New York City. My grandfather hired three Finnish sisters, registered nurses, who each took an eight-hour shift. These ladies were attractive, immaculate in every way, and consummate professionals. We all felt blessed to have such good care for Goldie. We insisted that the sisters join us for meals and feel like part of the family.

A few weeks before Grandma died, while she was still home, the sisters left abruptly for Finland, saying their mother had fallen ill and needed them. Within a few days, my grandma's condition worsened, and she was hospitalized and then passed away.

A few months later, my grandfather realized that things were missing from his home, mainly jewelry and clothing of my grandmother's. Thousands of dollars' worth of items had disappeared. The nurses had taken the stuff once they saw their job was soon to end. They must have planned it as impeccably as everything else they did. We were too frozen in our grief to try to find or prosecute these women.

Still, it was a painful and disillusioning experience. We decided that no matter what they had taken, they had given our loved one good care and for that we would always be thankful.

My grandmother's really good jewelry was in a vault. She left me some beautiful things that I remember her wearing a lot because these items were her "day" jewelry. Sometimes she visits me in a dream, and I hug her and tell her how much I miss her. I always feel her close.

Cody

I wouldn't be the person I am had I not had Cody in my life.

She was my first soul mate. Sadly, I don't even know her last name.

I can't visit her graveside because I don't know where or even if she's buried, but I think she is because she belonged to a church in Harlem.

Cody worked for my mother's parents, my grandma Goldie and grandpa Lou, as their maid. She worked full time, Monday through Friday. She lived in Harlem.

When I was still a baby, my grandmother sent her to help my mother take care of me. Even before I can remember it, Cody loved me. She loved the baby I was and always told me so as I got older. She loved me purely and not because she got paid to take care of me. I felt her love every time I was with her. When we went to my grandparents' home for dinner or a visit, I would run into the kitchen first, wanting to see Cody and get the big hug she always gave me. I'd hug her back and feel so happy.

Cody confided things to me. She belonged to a church in Harlem that had faith healings. She would tell me about seeing people who were crippled walk after being touched by the priest. Her faith was deep and rich. It drew me to her. Her eyes held mine when we talked. Our love for each other was singular and special. To my grandparents and parents, Cody was "the help"—a term they used matter-of-factly, like saying "refrigerator" or "bathroom." For me she was a mountain of spiritual nourishment. She came from the Carolinas—I'm not sure if it was North or South—and she spoke with a cadence and a way of pronouncing words and expressions that I still like to mimic today. If she liked coffee ice cream, for example, she would say,

"I loves me my coffee ice cream!"

Cody had a daughter named Gladys, who had a baby named Patricia. When I was about six, Cody came to take care of me on a weekend, and she brought Gladys and Patricia. I put Patricia in my doll carriage and wheeled her around. I loved having a baby in my home. I was an only child and longed for a sister or brother.

One time, Cody told me that she had asked my grandfather for a raise. She'd been earning sixty-five dollars per week for many years. He turned her down. She told me this not to turn me against my grandfather at all, just to share her life with me. I understood that she was glad to have her job even without the raise. Still, she knew she deserved one. She was a superb housekeeper. Cody went about her job with a professionalism and expertise that has continued to be a model for me of how to do anything in life. When she dusted, she hummed as if she were on roller skates. She cleaned everywhere, not just the visible surfaces. Her uniform was always washed, ironed, and starched, right down to the bow of her apron. Her pride and thorough work ethic was firstly for herself. She would expect nothing less from herself.

While she was excellent at cleaning, her cooking immortalized her for me.

She not only taught me how to cook and bake; she gave me the passion for it that she had. I was twenty-two and pregnant when I first asked her how she made the delicious dishes she served at my grandparents' home. She patiently told me every part of the process for each recipe she gave me—nuances she'd discovered over the years, special must-have ingredients, possible problems to avoid. She used vermouth in a chicken dish, but it had to be Noilly Prat Extra Dry—no other brand would yield that lovely broth—just as an example. She said I had to bake with Swans Down flour because it made cakes and cookies light and spongy. She told me only chicken fat would work to sauté the livers for chopped chicken liver. My mother and grandmother had no interest in these skills. I did and was blessed to have Cody as my teacher.

Cody had a sister named Lucretia who worked for my mother's sister, my aunt Cynthia. Lucretia was also an amazing cook with her own special dishes. One was her corn fritters, which she served with Vermont maple syrup. Lucretia and Cody had a mild sibling rivalry. Cody would say to me, "Don't you be askin' Cretia for no recipes because she will acts like she's giving it, but she will leave out one ingredient—she always do. Then, when yours don't come out like hers, she acts like she don't understand how that could be!"

I was twenty-two when I gave birth to my daughter, Judy. I invited Cody to come visit and see the baby. When she first came into my apartment, she automatically headed for the kitchen. I stopped her and told her she was my guest. I brought her into my daughter's room and asked her what I could get for her to eat or drink. Awkwardly, she accepted my offer of ice tea. Even now as I write this, some forty-four years later, I am tearing up, remembering how joyful it was for me to serve her for once. She held my six-week-old baby in a calm and soothing manner that I borrowed from her afterward. She laid Judy tummy down across her wide lap and gently rocked her thick, solid legs up and down, and my daughter allowed it, like a sailboat buoyed by the sea.

Shortly after this visit, my husband was given a work transfer to Los Angeles, and within two weeks we were living in Beverly Hills. I never saw Cody again. She passed away about a year later. Neither my mother nor my grandfather Lou thought to tell me. I had been trying to reach Cody at my grandfather's apartment.

Usually during the day, she was there and answered the phone "Frieds' residence." After several attempts where the phone just rang and rang, I called my mother to ask where Cody was and why wasn't she answering the phone. There was a palpable beat or two, a silence that I can still recall, before my mother said that Cody had died about a month or so before. I started to yell and cry and asked why no one had let me know. My mother said she was sorry; it just had not occurred to her that I needed to know.

I was so young then and going through my own life changes living in Los Angeles—learning to drive, being a new mother—and so I grieved Cody's death quietly to myself, not trying to find out where she was buried or even what her whole name was. Too many years later, when both my mother and grandfather were gone, I realized that Gladys and Patricia might very well be living somewhere, and I felt so utterly frustrated that I didn't know how to contact them. I still have not given up hope that somehow I will be able to connect with one of them.

I don't go many days without thinking of Cody. I love cleaning my home or baking in my kitchen because I commune with her when I do, almost feeling her warm, heavy breath on my face.

Lucy (My Mother, Lucille Fried Butterman Graham)

It's humbling to realize that one's parent was also a person separate from being the parent. I am thinking of my mother, who started out in life as Lucille Fried, the daughter and firstborn child of Goldie and Lou Fried. Lucille was born on February 21, 1923, almost nine months to the day after her parents had married. When Lucille was four, her sister and only sibling, Cynthia, was born. They were sisterly to each other and respectful, but no deeply emotional bond existed between them in that they were very different. By the time my mother was a teen, she felt she was somewhat of a black sheep in the family. She was distant and aloof and did not feel seen or heard by her parents. Both daughters were given classical piano lessons and were raised with the expectation that they would marry, keep lovely homes, and become mothers. My mother veered away from Mozart and Beethoven and became an avid jazz fan. She loved Louis Armstrong and Billie Holliday. She was on her own there. When, at twenty, she met the love of her life, her parents and his parents put a stop to the relationship because he was only eighteen, and those two years were just not acceptable then. After that, my mother pretty much gave up for a while. She met my father, newly home from fighting in the South Pacific in World War II, and married him because they had some lusty chemistry and because her parents were on her case with their expectations. Quite quickly she found herself pregnant with me, not planned but certainly welcome news to her parents and to my father's parents, if not wholly to them. They found an apartment, and my father went to work for his father-in–law. Suddenly my mother was living the life she was supposed to lead.

I was born one month before my parents' first wedding anniversary. A nurse was also engaged to help my mother with me. The nurse was strict. When I would cry from my crib and my mother tried to go and pick me up, the nurse would stop her, saying, "Just when you think you cannot take it another moment, she'll stop," and in fact, so my mother told me, I did. The nurse left when I was eighteen months old.

My mother was unhappy during this period. Her marriage to my father was not turning out to be that great. They were not truly in love or soul mates, so when the novelty of their lust was over, two strangers were living together with a small child.

Finally, after almost ten years, my mother wanted a divorce. Once single and in her early thirties, her life really began. She immersed herself back in the world of jazz music. She took jazz piano lessons, bought lots of records, and got a secretarial job working for a manager of jazz artists. The first summer she was single, in 1957, when I was nine, she spent a few weeks at the new School of Jazz in Lenox, Massachusetts, while I was at sleepaway summer camp. She had piano lessons with jazz great Oscar Peterson. Here are some of her comments about that experience when asked by the school to write something for its student comments and testimonials column:

> It has been the most unique and inspiring single event in my life to have been exposed to the personality and performance of the faculty... I spent more time with Oscar Peterson than any of the others and can't say too much about his greatness as a human being, performer, and teacher...His advice to the small ensemble actually formed an ideal democratic credo that could be carried into all other phases of life...I feel that now I will approach my playing with more of an inner ear to the fullest expression of what I want to say. I feel that I will explore and stretch my own resources and reach a place in playing that I hardly knew existed before coming here.

My mother's love of jazz and enthusiasm at this time for that world was meaningful and necessary for her. I can understand this today, but at that time, I resented all the attention the jazz got and felt somehow in competition with it for her love. In the 1950s, if you asked little girl me if I liked jazz I would tell you I hated it. In adulthood, however, I have come to passionately love all of the music and musicians my mother had. Ironically, it brings her close to me every time I listen to a piece of music she had discovered back in the fifties and sixties. Much of it is on my iPod today.

Men were very attracted to her, and she had an active social life. Lots of the men she dated fell for her, but she remained cool. Then she fell hard for a man named Chip, and he broke her heart. Eventually, she tried marriage one more time, when she was fifty-two, but sadly that relationship fell apart within a few years. By her midfifties, she was done being the sexy divorcée whose dance card was always filled.

Her next chapter involved moving from New York City to Fort Lauderdale, Florida, and starting a consignment furniture business with one of her long-time best girlfriends. The business was quite successful for a number of years, during which time they opened a total of five stores. At that point, they had spread themselves too thin and also were getting tired or just bored with furniture, and so the business closed shop. Still, it was a terrific experience for my mother and gave her an identity as a businesswoman who could be her own boss. Prior to this, she'd only held secretarial-type jobs when she worked. Because of her father's wealth and ability to help her out financially, she was never hard-pressed to earn money to put food on the table or a roof over her head. In addition to the furniture business, my mother also became an expert knitter after moving to Florida. She made gorgeous sweaters that she sold on consignment to local boutiques. She also knitted sweaters for me, and I loved getting and wearing them.

My mother was a major reader of books. I cannot ever remember her not being in a book. She loved well-written novels and adored Norman Mailer, Doris Lessing, Saul Bellow, and John Barth, just to name a few. She loved having her mind and intellect stimulated—for her it was a drug, a turn-on.

I have her entire collection of Modern Library books that she brought into her marriage to my father. The books have been on a shelf in every home in which I have lived since I was born. I have read many of them but love that I still have ones to discover.

When my mother was newly divorced from my father and just finding herself, she explored all kinds of things that spoke to her. She almost put herself and ten-year-old me on a macrobiotic diet because she read about its health benefits. When I was in high school, she was casting my *I Ching*. She was fascinated by Timothy Leary's experimentation with psychedelic drugs like LSD. The idea of expanding one's mind excited her. She almost signed up to be part of a doctor's LSD lab group but then got cold feet. Later on, she was glad of this. The drugs were strong and the results too unpredictable to be safe for many users. My mother learned graphology and thereafter always checked the handwriting of her friends, the men she dated, and even my friends if I showed her one of their letters.

My mother had been classically trained on the piano as a child, so even as she embraced learning and playing jazz compositions, she also always played classical pieces. Her sight-reading of music was first-rate, and she could sit at the piano, open a piano sonata by Mozart or Beethoven, and play it beautifully with her first read. After my father moved out, my mother and I would spend enjoyable nights at the piano, singing Bach chorales or Broadway songs that she would have the sheet music to. I always wished I could sight-read like she did, but that particular skill was not one I could master, even though over the decades, on and off, I took piano lessons. I have a very good ear for music and can improvise a song I've heard on the piano, but to play a classical piece I love takes a lot of time and practice for me.

In the summer of 1987, my mother's father, Lou, decided late in his life to sell his Fifth Avenue apartment. By then, he was living in West Palm Beach and hardly coming to the city at all. He invited me, my mother, and her sister, Cynthia, to come and claim whatever we wanted before he had the rest of the contents sold by an estate furniture agent. I came in from the Boston area, where I was living at that time, and met my mother and Aunt Cynthia at Grandpa Lou's apartment.

Neither my mother nor my aunt wanted much, but I did, having fond and nostalgic memories of the dining table and chairs, as an example.

My mother and Cynthia's mother, my grandma Goldie, had a Steinway spinet piano, which she had loved and played while she was alive. As we stood with the furniture agent in Grandpa's apartment, I asked my mother and aunt which one of them would take Grandma's piano. My aunt had a lovely piano in her apartment, and my mother had gotten herself an inexpensive one when she'd moved to Florida, so they both said they didn't want the piano. I had a Baldwin piano in my home, which was my twenty-first birthday present from my father's parents, so I didn't need the piano; however, I knew it was not leaving the family. I looked my mother in the eye and told her she absolutely had to take her mother's piano and get rid of the inexpensive one (I think it was a Yamaha).

At first, she wasn't inclined to because the piano would have to be moved from New York City to Boca Raton. I told her that if she didn't take it, I would move it up to the Boston area and pay to store it rather than let it go. At that point, she said she would take it. After it arrived, she thanked me for making her take it. She loved playing it, and when my daughter, Judy, and I visited her, she would play songs from Broadway shows, and we would sing along. One of her favorites was *The Phantom of the Opera.* She also wrote a few songs of her own, which she would play and sing for us. One was called "Through the Eyes of Love" and began with the lyric "Look at me through the eyes of love."

When my mother passed away, the only thing Judy wanted was her grandma's piano, which was ironic since I had wanted it to stay in the family because it was my grandma's piano. I had it moved from Florida to New Jersey and stored it for a number of years until it could be put in Judy's home. By then, she was married and had a baby. Now, that baby, Eve, is almost thirteen and beautifully plays her great-grandma Lucy's and great-great-grandma Goldie's piano. The word *joy* does not adequately describe the feeling I have when Eve plays that piano.

My mother was known mostly in the second half of her life as Lucy instead of Lucille. She was a unique person on this planet, separate from being my mother. As a child, I had needs that were not always met by her. It was a difficult period in her as-yet-unrealized life. While those years for me felt one way, they felt another way for her. Understanding this is sobering.

When I was an adult woman with a child of my own, my mother embraced being a grandmother and also circled back around to motherhood. She doted on seeing Judy and me. She planned holidays and birthdays with us. She sent all kinds of gifts to us for no reason. She and Judy had a very special relationship. My mother would tell me that she felt "most heard" by Judy, who is and has always been an incredibly kind and compassionate human being. For my mother, who did not at all feel heard or seen for who she was growing up, this was profoundly meaningful.

The circle of life means that the child becomes the parent, and so, when my mother became terminally ill with leukemia, I took a leave from my job and spent her last weeks with her. Judy got excused from classes at college to be with her as well.

We were both with my mother when she drew her last breath on November 17, 1992.

Author's Note

Several years after my mother passed away, I wrote a piece entitled "Melon Balls." I envisioned my mother standing at a microphone in front of an audience performing it as an autobiographical monologue that she had written about episodes in her life that truly happened to her.

I actually did perform it like this at a reading in New York City's Knitting Factory and was deeply gratified by the enthusiastic response it received from the audience.

Melon Balls

I'm having a melon ball, my favorite drink. It's more like dessert. The ingredients are sours, Midori liqueur, which is green like a honeydew, and vodka. I like Absolut, absolutely! It's five o'clock in the afternoon, cocktail hour. I only have two, tops. I'm not really a drinker; that's not my thing, like Häagen-Dazs coffee ice cream, which holds me hostage. But melon balls are festive and give me a surge of hope late in the day, like catching the first hue of the sunrise, which I would never get to see since I don't do dawn!

In the sixties, I drank Dewar's on the rocks like my parents. It's about the only way I was like them. I don't drink when I'm dining. I don't actually dine. I eat and enjoy it most of the time, but dining is more organized and implies family, husband, date.

I usually have dinner home by myself while I watch *Jeopardy!* or out with a girlfriend. Once in a while, a married friend brings her husband along, which is fine with me. I have nothing against other women's husbands. I have nothing against men as a group, and I don't think they make every decision from the perspective of their zippers. It's just that men come and go as they please a lot more than women do.

One man came and went right on top of me! That was very upsetting and embarrassing. Herb was fun, and we'd been on a few dates. It was the free-to-be-me early seventies, so I invited him to spend the night. He was a decent lover for an insurance adjuster, newly separated. He called me Gloria a few times by mistake, said it was his wife's name, and I understood that. In the morning he wanted more attention, and even though I'm not a morning person, I felt friendly, so we had a second interlude. Herb was more passionate than the night before and groaned and moaned having his orgasm. Then, the life sort of went out of him, which I thought was par for the course. But he was not moving at all or breathing or lifelike.

"Herb," I said, giving his shoulders a rustle. "Herb," I yelled, shaking him, but he just slumped to my side. I was terrified, so I called my daughter, and my son-in-law answered. He said he'd be right over but to call an ambulance. Herb died of a heart attack. It could have been any woman he was with. His time was up, period. And he died happy, I always said to myself afterward, to lessen my guilt, I guess. But it wasn't my fault! Guilt is to women what water is to fish. We can rise above it and smell the air for about a second. It starts with being female. The guilt of her, you know, Eve. Poor, innocent Adam was just meandering around the Garden of Eden when she offered him the forbidden fruit. Now I sound like my daughter. She says the Bible story is just a metaphor for our special fruity spot between our legs. We're all temptresses except for that other famous lady, Mary. She's a mom, but she's a virgin. Her fruit stayed forbidden, so she can be worshipped.

Anyhow, that's all behind me now. I'm not guilty, and I'm not a seductress. I'm off men since I divorced my second husband, Bart, fourteen years ago. It was a short union, less than two years. We married in 1975, almost twenty years after my first divorce.

Bart taught music, and I played piano. We had a jammin' courtship, and in hindsight, I should have kept that going like I did with the other men I had dated, even when they proposed, but I wanted to try living happily ever after one more time. I was fifty-two by then. Bart changed after we married. He began to criticize me as if I were an imperfect score of music. I was not into that.

The man I wanted to marry originally was two years younger than I. At the time, the early 1940s, that wasn't OK. My parents were upset, his parents were afraid he'd quit school, and between them they killed it. They felt justified because I hadn't done what I was supposed to do; I hadn't picked right, so I had to be corrected before it became a bigger mistake. Larry, that was his name, didn't understand what was happening. He figured we could just reconnect a little later on, when two years seemed shorter than his being eighteen and my being twenty.

He said, "Let's just go along with our parents now so when we end up together, we'll still be talking to them." I knew that would never happen, that they'd already won. I wasn't supposed to make a fuss, push, so I didn't.

Eventually I married a man I liked kissing, six months after we met. Ed was two years older than I. My parents were relieved. At twenty-three, my chances had declined, and the window of opportunity was only open by a crack. So they went into high gear having my wedding at the Pierre hotel—men in top hats and tails, me in white satin, ice-sculpture cupids, glorious food served on white bone china, a fourteen-piece band prompting everyone to the dance floor.

I got through ten years of marriage, from 1946 to 1956. I really wanted it to work even if my husband wasn't Larry. Eddie and I tried to have something. Maybe that was the problem. It wasn't there on its own. I got pregnant right away and unplanned, and so we had to get down to family business. I'm not joking. My husband of a few months went to work for my father, and that didn't help matters between us other than financial. My dad was tough, and my husband wasn't. That's all pretty ancient history now.

I did come to after my divorce. I got reacquainted with myself. I was definitely America's first swinging single, since it was 1957, and the phrase didn't even hit until the sixties! Men could not get enough of me, to my utter disbelief and delight. I was a brunette during my marriage, but I became a redheaded divorcée. Not auburn, r-e-d! Half the men I dated called me "Red." At the time, I wanted to start a magazine for singles called *Solo*. I should have; there was nothing like it then; I was ahead of the times.

I didn't do the magazine. I was too busy going on dates. Not that I had any interest in meeting another husband then. I was just enjoying men's company. It was my job. During the day, I was a secretary, but that was boring. My fun work was seeing guys like Jerry, a sweet man who was vice president in charge of something at Saks. He gave me a charge card that said I was his wife so I could shop wholesale at any Saks store. Now I did not ask him to do that! I have never been into stuff that way. It was a nice gesture, and I thanked him for it, but I would have slept with him anyhow for as long as I did.

I can't be bought—not with things. You get into my head, my intellect, that's another story. Larry got there. We connected effortlessly like one beating heart, stimulated mind, and happy soul. Some people never experience that.

I did once, when I was twenty, for six months. And I was right about Larry, about us. I know because I ran into him fifteen years after our parting. I was standing at the Sixty-Seventh Street bus stop on Madison Avenue. He came next to me, and instantly we said each other's name. Our eyes locked just like they had in the past. We stood talking while buses came and went. I told him about my marriage, my divorce, my daughter. He said he'd met his wife a few years after we broke up and that they'd been married for twelve years and had two children. He seemed happy with his life, but our chemistry was still there, almost knocking us off the curb! I felt it, and he looked like he did too. It was so good being next to him, getting easy inside like I always did with him, that I didn't care if he was married, a father, anything. I was ready to be with him. I didn't say that out loud; I didn't have to. Finally, he said, "Lucille, I was heartbroken when I couldn't be with you—you know that—and seeing you right now is stirring those feelings in me. But I love my wife very much. I'm with her in life just like I would have been with you." I whispered something unoriginal like, 'I understand, Larry. Take care,' then turned and walked up Madison. At Seventy-Second Street, I hailed a taxi and sat rigid the whole ride. I made it up to my apartment, and when I was in—my coat was still on—I dropped to the floor sobbing.

"I was right," I kept gasping. "I was right about Larry. I picked a real good man who would have been true to me."

My Father, Edward Butterman

My father, Edward Butterman was born on February 23, 1921, to Sara and Herman Butterman. He would be their only child. The family lived in the Grand Concourse section of the Bronx. His parents doted on him, their little prince.

Herman, a Jewish immigrant from Latvia, worked on Wall Street and had begun accumulating an impressive amount of money. In 1929, when Ed was eight, the market crashed, and Herman saw his "fortune" gone in a day. Herman had an emotional breakdown as a result and was absent from the home for six months, recovering at some kind of facility. My facts on this are sketchy. I had heard as a child about my grandfather's bleeding ulcer in his thirties when the market crashed because he was so freaked out about losing something like $60,000, but I had never heard until my dad, at ninety, mentioned that when he was eight, his father was suddenly gone from the home for six months with no explanation from my grandmother. My father told me this when we were having a rare and special father-daughter lunch. He seemed still stunned by that long-ago absence as he related it. I regret now that I didn't ask him more about that incident. He seemed himself to have only a few details: that his father was gone and then six months later he came back, period.

My earliest memories of my father are at our first apartment 1101 on the Upper West Side of New York City. We lived there from my birth until I was eight. I remember my father then as a handsome young man with a sense of humor but also a temper. When he found me amusing, he smiled and cajoled me; when I was fresh or misbehaved, he cursed me and came toward me with his belt, but my mother always intervened and said, "No, Eddie, please don't," and he never did. Still, when his temper showed, I felt scared. He was wound tightly, unlike my soft, malleable mother.

I knew he was different from my mom and me. He shaved his face every day in their bathroom after he showered. I would go in sometimes to watch him do this. He had a towel wrapped around his waist like a skirt. He'd lift one leg and place it on the rim of the bathtub for balance, and I could see between his lifted leg and his standing one part of his genitalia where the towel pulled away. I had absolutely no idea what that was and no need to ask about it. It just fascinated me for no reason other than it was not what my mom or I had in that spot on our bodies.

I just knew it had to do with him being the dad, not the mom.

My father ate a soft-boiled egg for breakfast in the kind of eggcup where you eat it right out of the shell. He ate lamb chops for dinner and mixed mashed potatoes and spinach together. I watched him a lot for cues, for whether or not I was pleasing him. I seemed to exist to do so. We watched baseball and Westerns on television together. We loved Sid Caesar's *Your Show of Shows* at night.

His temper could also be spent on my mother. He could be short with her or find fault with her. He was never abusive, however, and his anger usually had some degree of legitimacy in that I was doing something annoying or my mother was acting unintelligently about something. At least that is how it seemed to me then.

The fear factor for my mother and myself was not extreme; it just had its own dose of tension so that our home did not feel particularly calm or sweet.

My father and mother divorced when I was nine, and my father moved out.

After that, I saw him mainly on Sundays. He no longer had to discipline me because our visits were more like dates—going ice-skating, to theater, to dinner, or to see my grandparents.

When I was thirteen, he told me he had met a French woman named Denise and they were in love. He moved in with her, and they lived together on Seventy-Second Street and Park Avenue. She was very aloof toward me the few times I saw her. My father did not make any attempt for her and me to know each other or spend any time together. His life was his alone, except for the time he spent with me on his designated visitation schedule. Other than at these times, I was not part of his life or the people in it. Dad and Denise ended their relationship after eight years, and she moved back to France. He seemed OK about the breakup.

A few years later, my father fell in love with Ellen, with whom he would eventually marry and spend the rest of his life. By that time, I was married, had a baby, and lived in Los Angeles while they were in New York City. Ellen had two daughters from her first marriage, and my father became an involved stepdad to them, especially the younger one, still at home in the middle of high school. He seemed to be able to be there for his stepdaughter in ways he had not been for me.

He was older, settled, and in love, and his home life was happy, so having a teenage stepdaughter who was not close to her own dad gave my father the chance to meet the needs for her that he was not able to meet for me. Saying this today has nothing to do with how it felt to me at the time. I was aware of his new family, and despite having by then a family of my own, I still felt cheated since I had not had my dad at home during my high school years.

The family he made with Ellen and her daughters was the family he had for the rest of his life, another forty-plus years. I had not been his priority before he met Ellen, and I was not after.

Over the years, as my first two marriages failed, my father did console me and give me fatherly wisdom about men and romance as I navigated through dates I hoped would lead me to my own soul mate. When I met Alan, however, my father did not ever seem to be totally thrilled for me, even though I had indeed found the love of my life. I don't know why exactly this was, but it was, and it made me sad. My father never seemed to "get" how wonderful Alan was for me and how happy we were.

When my mother passed away in 1992, I inherited money to which Ellen felt entitled. She had my father ask me to buy them a condo to live in that I would actually own, but I did not want to do that and told my father so. He seemed fine with this, but a few weeks later I got a scathing letter from Ellen telling me what a horrible, uncaring daughter I was to deny my father this condo.

I immediately called my father, read him the letter, which he had not known she'd written, and told him I would not be speaking to her again. Thus began an eight-year period during which I did not speak to Ellen but still did have monthly phone visits with my dad. By this time, I was back in New York City, while they were in the San Francisco area of California.

At eighty-four, my father suffered a stroke, which left him unable to swallow. My daughter, Judy, and I dropped everything and went to California to be with him in the hospital. Even though I had not spoken to Ellen for years, we reconnected in support of my father and have remained connected ever since.

My father was able to fully recover and started swallowing again about three months later. He lived for another eight years and passed away on December 20, 2012, a few months before what would have been his ninety-second birthday.

My father did not want and did not have a funeral. We did have a gathering of family and friends to celebrate his life at the home he and Ellen shared in Santa Rosa, California. I read the following notes to the group and also read notes that my daughter, Judy, had written and emailed to me. Below are our remembrances.

Notes on My Father, Ed Butterman (1921–2012)

My dad, Ed Butterman, was the opposite of a klutz. He was suave, classy, and nuanced. He read people and situations and had a reliable gut he listened to.

In his early twenties, he joined the navy and saw action in World War II. His ship was in the South Pacific, and at one point a kamikaze pilot bombed the ship next to his. He also suffered a serious bout with dengue fever while in the South Pacific.

My dad was a real survivor, and once I asked him what it was like during the war, waking up and not knowing if he would live through the day. He told me he was not scared and just knew he would make it home.

My dad loved the good life: good wine; gourmet food; theater; music; literature. He was an avid reader. He took me to see *An Evening with Mike Nichols and Elaine May* on Broadway when I was ten, even though it was way beyond my years. Whether we were having a lunch visit or a dinner one, we dined in lovely New York City restaurants. When I was twenty-one, he made me try escargot. I drew the line at sweetbreads.

He didn't let the fact that I was not a son cramp his style. When I was six or seven, my dad excitedly told me he was taking me to see the Giants. We took a train out, and the whole trip I was so scared, thinking these were real giants, like the one in the "Jack and the Beanstalk" story. When we got to the baseball stadium, I was quite relieved.

My dad was always honest with me, or, as he put it, "brutally frank." Even as a kid, I knew if I asked him a question about anything I would get a straight answer.

My parents divorced in 1956, when I was nine. For a number of years, my dad was a serial dater, but when he met Ellen, that was it. They truly were soul mates for the past forty-plus years.

Since 1970, my father and I have lived on opposite coasts, so much of our time together has been spent having phone visits. I will deeply miss hearing his luscious, gravelly voice as he dispensed his own brand of fatherly wisdom that went beyond even his ninety-one years.

May he rest in peace as he does in my heart.

Notes on Grandpa Ed, by Judy Hammett

My grandpa Ed, a.k.a. Gramps, as I fondly called him, was like an old friend whom you rarely see, but whom you click with instantly the moment you are reunited.

We could go for long periods without contact, and then when we came together, it was as if no time had passed at all. I could always just relax with him, for Gramps was a seasoned, wide-open man who would not judge or throw stones about anything. He'd seen it all, done it all, had no role he expected either of us to play.

We'd sit together in our rare but precious meetings and talk like long-lost buddies. He'd set his steady blue gaze on me, speaking with candor about his life, his memories, answering my questions—always full of humor and that wonderful, easy, straight-shooting style that was all his own. There was a timelessness about our kinship that carried us through this life and will continue on in my heart forever.

I will miss his loving, ironic smile and direct address "How are ya, Jude?" and the engaged, passionate exchanges that would ensue between us. I am grateful for those gems, those special windows we had to share the ins and outs of life. I will miss him and miss having him see Eve grow and evolve. I know they would have delighted each other.

My husband, Dave, Eve, and I are with you all in heart and spirit. We carry the memory of Grandpa forward with love and joy.

Buried Truth

Terror in a ten-year-old body is numbing, completely. The body doesn't tremble, and the heart beats no faster. The body doesn't, period. It freezes automatically, like a light switch being flicked off. I know because I experienced this phenomenon when I was ten.

For the first twenty-five years or so after the experience, I didn't even recall the event that had terrified me—it was totally buried. I'm certainly not alone here—so that means countless child molesters are never identified or accused and dealt with by anyone. They just do their molesting under the radar because their young victims don't remember, sometimes ever, what was done to them. Some children do talk about their experience when it is taking place. That's when a molester can be apprehended if the adults being told believe the child. I hope that is always the case. Children really can't lie about behavior they don't have any knowledge of or words for unless it is actually done to them. They aren't born knowing about sexual behavior, and for me at least it didn't have the label of "sex" because I did not know that word at the time. It was an odd game I was asked to be playing that just felt terrifyingly wrong, part of the terror being that I was ten and games were fun but this didn't feel anything like that, for no reason I could identify.

When I was ten, I was living with my mother (my father had moved out due to their divorce) at a very lovely white-glove building, now a landmark on Seventy-Second Street and Central Park West. Just a few blocks up was an equally beautiful white-glove building on Seventy-Fourth Street and Central Park West.

My two friends, Paula and Beth, lived in the Seventy-Fourth Street building. The three of us spent lots of time together at one of our apartments. We were allowed to walk the two blocks back and forth to one another's homes by ourselves. Our buildings had attended elevators as well as doormen, and we knew these people on a first-name basis. The man that worked the elevator at Paula and Beth's building during the day I will call Anthony because, even now, saying his actual name, no less printing it, is scary. Paula and Beth lived on the same side of their building and took that elevator up to their apartments on different floors. They and I were frequently on that elevator, coming or going from visits to one another. One day when I was in the elevator going to Paula or Beth's floor and alone with Anthony, he stopped the elevator between floors and turned to me. A large pink thing was protruding from the middle of his uniform. I had no understanding at that time that it was part of him. He said he had a "new friend" for me to shake hands with and told me to shake hands with the pink thing. He may have guided my hand—I don't remember for sure—but I do know that I felt I had to do it. He said it was our "shaking-hands game," and it was a secret. In the days to follow, he did this again with me and either Paula or Beth or both of them. The three of us talked about the secret "game" Anthony made us play. We even giggled nervously about it. That was part of the fear for me. At the time, I instinctively felt I should not tell anyone about it. My mouth couldn't be pried open to tell. I don't know why I knew not to tell; I just did in a visceral way that felt like survival. Beth, however, did eventually tell her mother. Anthony was fired on the spot. My mother asked me about it, but I don't recall what, if anything, I said. What I do remember clearly is that Beth, Paula, and I walked to our school, PS 87, together—about six city blocks—and after Beth told and Anthony got fired, we would tremble walking to school, scared he was mad at us for getting him in trouble and waiting to "get us" as we walked. We'd stick together, looking ahead and behind and into doorways, sure he'd jump out of one and hurt us for what we did. We felt guilty for costing him his job. This occurred while we were in the fifth grade together. When school let out for summer break, we went to different sleepaway camps, and we were not in the same sixth-grade classroom—just as it turned out, not having anything to do with what had happened to us.

I buried the entire incident deep inside me, so deeply it could have been deleted forever. It was gone for some twenty-five years. Then, when I was thirty-five, I heard a celebrity on television talking about being molested as a child by one of her relatives but only *just* remembering it in her adulthood. Some people were skeptical of her account since she'd never before given it. They accused her of lying, trying to get publicity or back at relatives she just didn't particularly like. This deeply and quite immediately affected me because I knew it could happen. I thought about writing to the celebrity to tell her this as I realized it *had* happened to me! As the memory of that time surfaced in my consciousness suddenly and fully, I started to shake uncontrollably, my teeth chattering as if it were freezing, which it wasn't at all; I was living in Southern California at the time. For several months, I couldn't say what I had remembered out loud. When I finally did, I shook the whole time, and I could never say the elevator man's name. It was years before I could talk about the incident without starting to shake. I can now but do get that body halt with the thought of his name. My gut starts to tighten even though I never saw "Anthony" again and he's almost certainly dead. I think about the fact that back then he was fired, but I don't think he was legally apprehended. We children didn't have to make any formal account to anyone. I don't even know if there were laws on the books then that dealt with pedophiles, it being 1957. Were we the last children "Anthony" played his shaking-hands game with?

2016 Author's Update

An amazing thing has happened within the past few months. I have reconnected, all these fifty-eight years later, with Paula and Beth as part of a reunion being planned for PS 87 fifth and sixth graders from 1957 to 1958 by some of our fellow classmates! I had not talked or communicated with Paula since sixth grade and Beth since college in the 1960s!

This has enabled me to revisit the "Anthony" chapter with them. The irony is that we each have a different memory of what happened. Beth thinks it was hilarious and says she talks about that crazy elevator man with his exposing-himself games all the time and that for her, it is her funniest stand-up-type anecdote to tell friends, who find it most amusing!

Paula remembers that she thought it was weird and it made her uncomfortable, but she was not traumatized in the way that I felt I was. Her memory is that it first happened to her and me together. My memory is that it first happened to me alone.

What we all remember is the abuse, although at the time, we wouldn't have called it that. Unlike Beth and Paula, I truly did bury the whole of it for all those years, and I for sure shook all over, teeth chattering like I was in Alaska instead of Los Angeles when the memory of it came back to me in the early 1980s, when I was in my midthirties.

Thumb Habit

As a child, I sucked my left thumb every night to fall asleep. I had a routine that went with the sucking. I would lie on my right side beneath the covers and slide my right arm under my pillow. My head rested on it, facing the wall my bed was placed against. Once settled this way, I would raise my hand to my mouth. I'd suck my thumb while my left index finger gently rubbed the spot between my upper lip and nose. Intermittently and quite rhythmically, I would stop the rubbing and instead use my left index and middle fingers to make a crease in the pillowcase that the fingers would then press to the side in a tiny but swift motion that made an audible snap.

Sometimes, I would repeatedly do the snapping part, needing to hear the little clicks in the lifeless quiet. Other nights, I would rub under my nose longer, needing the caress of skin on skin. But always I sucked. My thumb fit in my mouth as naturally as my teeth.

When I was eight, we moved, and I had a new room and bed, but I still maintained my nocturnal rite. Sucking my thumb was the constant, reliable part of my life. I could count on my thumb to be there just for me.

Most of my time was spent not sucking my thumb because I only did so at bedtime. Still, each minute my thumb was pressed securely against the roof of my mouth meant much to me for the next whole day.

When I was ten, I was taken to an orthodontist to see if I needed braces. His name was Dr. Unger, and he was the ugliest man I'd ever seen. He had no hair or eyebrows, blotchy skin, and eyes that looked like big, wet marbles rolling behind round wire-framed glasses. For my first visit, he took impressions of my teeth by having me bite into U-shaped trays filled with soft, gummy stuff.

When I came for the second appointment, I sat in the chair, and Dr. Unger showed me what looked like a pair of white, chalky false teeth.

"This is your impression, Joanne. See how your top teeth overshoot your bottom ones?" He tried to wedge his pinky behind the front teeth of the impression to illustrate too much space there.

"I don't have buck teeth. I know kids who have buck teeth, and mine aren't," I informed him. He grinned with the benevolence of a missionary.

"Yes, well, thank goodness your teeth don't jut out more, or we'd have tons of work to do. But those front teeth of yours should touch the bottom teeth for a healthy, well-placed bite, so we've got to pull them back with a brace we'll fit across your top teeth."

"OK," I said, thinking I'd seen other girls with a silver band like that.

"But first, before any of that, we've got to stop the problem of why your teeth protrude." I looked at him, wondering what the problem could be. "You're still sucking your thumb, aren't you?"

"Yes, a little at night," I said, feeling like a puppy caught chewing the master's shoe.

"You have to stop, Joanne. You've got to break that habit. I'm going to help you."

He installed a piece of orthodontic equipment called a "thumb guard." It was a picket-fence-like chunk of metal hardware set in the roof of my mouth, occupying most of that space and anchored by metal rings that snugly fit over my back upper molars.

"I don't like this—take it out," I lisped, my tongue not functioning from its usual place.

"No, no, I can't do that. You'll get used to this, and it will come out eventually; it's temporary."

That first night, and for several thereafter, I tried to suck my thumb. I stuck it in each side of my mouth between my teeth and cheek. I put it in front of my top teeth. I was frantic, like a moth after dark at a lit window.

I snapped the pillowcase with my fingers while attempting to get my thumb positioned, but the clicks didn't work the way they had. I heard them in my ear, but the rest of me wasn't listening.

Eating was awkward, and my tongue got scratched in a few places until I got used to keeping it low, behind my bottom teeth. These discomforts were minor, ones I could handle. Not being able to suck my thumb made me feel as helpless as a turtle lying belly up.

I didn't tell anyone what I was going through. I'd never discussed my thumb sucking in any detail. I seemed the same to my friends and family. My life appeared to be just like it had been before I went to Dr. Unger.

A month passed, maybe two. I got used to the thumb guard. I went on despite it.

I went to see Dr. Unger, and he removed the guard. He said I was ready for the next brace, the band. I was thrilled but kept an even look on my face, afraid he might take it back and put the guard in again. I left his office as excited as I'd ever been. All I could think about was that I had won. I'd made it. I was still standing on the road tangled with gnarled roots Dr. Unger made me walk. I was like Superboy in my comic book. I could fly. Tonight, I thought gleefully, I can suck my thumb.

I got into bed that evening and began. I turned onto my right side, slid my right arm under the pillow, and brought my left hand to my mouth. It didn't feel right. My thumb felt big and in the way, like a foreign object that wasn't part of me. It tasted bitter. I tried to rub and suck. The rubbing was OK, but the sucking made me gag. It was like being forced to do it for the first time and needing to reject it. I rested my left hand on the pillow. I could barely see it in the darkness. I lay there missing my thumb like a lost best friend.

I hadn't won at all, I thought, starting to cry. I hadn't gotten through anything. I was changed, separated permanently from my thumb. I sobbed myself to sleep that night and for many to come, wanting to have my thumb back the way I'd had it, wanting my parents back together the way they had been, grieving what was irretrievable.

Broken Frogs

I hated being sent to sleepaway camp for eight weeks each summer, but it was the rule starting when I was five. We lived on the Upper West Side of New York City.

I was the only child. "You have to go to camp because the city is no place for a child in the summertime," my parents reasoned whenever I begged to stay at home. I'd cry and promise to be no bother, but their order stuck. I didn't understand why summer was so different from the rest of the time or why I couldn't go to a day camp, but my parents were nonnegotiable about this.

Getting on the bus for my first camp, Jack and Jill, the summer I was five was like having to go to school naked. My parents told me to be "brave," that "once you get there, you're going to have a good time." The camp was in Poughkeepsie, New York, about a two-hour drive from the city, but it felt very far away to me. Surrounded by eight other little girls, I felt alone in my bunk. I resented having to sleep in public with a bunch of strangers.

One of the girls in my bunk, Madeline, was deaf. In the middle of one night, I woke to hear her crying in a weird, honking-like way. I got up to follow the noise. She was at the bathroom sink with our counselor, who was washing out her mouth with soap, saying, "You don't talk right, and you've got to learn how to." I ran back to my bed, terrified by such cruelty. I befriended Madeline after that, but I wanted to go home even more.

Each summer after that, it was the same ritual. I begged not to have to go to camp while my parents stated the rule but some years said they'd pick a new, better camp. By the summer I was nine, I was starting my third camp, Somerset, in Maine. On parents' visiting weekend, we were divided into two teams and had a Singsong. Each team sang specific songs they'd written words to (the melodies were popular), and the counselors, who were the judges, scored each number performed. At the finish, the team with the most points won. That summer, the Thor team won. I was on the Bud team. When I found my parents in the audience afterward, my dad asked me if I was upset because my team had lost.

"No, I'm so glad that you and Mom are here. I don't care at all about losing."

I'd answered looking at their faces. Standing right next to them in that moment, I felt an immense and silent space engulfing us. I could make no sense of it; it just was.

Years later, I learned that my parents had lived apart that entire summer as a trial separation. Visiting day at camp was the first time they'd been together since I'd left. They'd sent me off and then started their trial. When I returned from camp, they were both at home to greet me as if nothing had changed, but within a few weeks, as I started fifth grade, I was told they were getting a divorce, and my dad moved out. He packed his clothes and went to a residential hotel on lower Park Avenue, one block from where his parents lived. He had a studio apartment, which consisted of an entry foyer leading to a sunken living room. An efficiency kitchenette and bathroom were off the foyer on the right. To the left was a closet with a Murphy bed that pulled down and out. The first time I went there, I looked all around and then asked, "Dad, where's your bedroom?" When he showed me the bed, stacked upright against the closet wall, I held back tears. He was all alone in one room.

The furniture wasn't even his.

The summer I was ten, I went to Camp Colang in Pennsylvania, another new camp. A lot of the kids knew one another from previous summers and picked up where they'd left off. I wanted to have friends and belong, so when a group of kids formed the Dissecting Frogs Club, I asked to join. "You'll have to be initiated," I was told. When it was my turn, I had to smash a baby frog about the size of my thumb with a big stone. Ahead of me, girls were giggling as they killed their frogs, which were caught, one at a time, as they popped up from the wet grass. Finally, I stepped up to the wooden bench that had been deemed the initiation table. I was handed the stone, stained from use. The leader of the club said, “I’m gonna put the frog down, and you gotta hit it real fast before he jumps off.”

I looked away from the bench and felt faint. I don’t recall for sure what happened next. I think I just shut my eyes and plunged the stone down, maybe on the frog, maybe not. I felt horrible inside and incredibly guilty, not just for myself but for all of us. I felt so sorry for the frogs. They had been hopping along like they were supposed to, being happy. I acted like I was having fun to fit in.

Eventually, I stopped going to club meetings. Still, when I closed my eyes at night, lying in bed in my bunk, I’d see a bloody, flattened smear that once was a little frog, and I’d wince and turn over, crying into my pillow.

We had one visiting day at camp Colang. It was a Sunday midway through the eight weeks, and even though it was the first summer since my parents’ divorce, they told me they would be coming together. No one at camp needed to know the truth. I was the only kid I knew who had divorced parents, it being the 1950s.

After my dad had moved out, I pretended he was still in our apartment. I would purposely say things like, “Hold on a minute—my dad’s asking me something” when on the phone with a friend. At school I’d say, “My dad had to help me with my math last night—it was so hard.” I was mortified to have divorced parents, like it meant something awful about me. Only my best friend, Robin, knew, and she said it didn’t matter; I was still her best friend.

My parents arrived at camp like they had all the summers before. My dad always smuggled in a salami, knife, and mustard for me, and my mom always looked around to see if the coast was clear to eat it! It was odd to see them together. For the past ten months, my dad had come on Sunday mornings to pick me up and take me ice-skating at Rockefeller Center and then on to his parents’ home for dinner. Then he’d leave me at the door to the apartment where I lived with my mom.

They were doing the same things they had in summers past, asking me what activities I liked, what friends had I made, but their voices didn’t seem connected to their throats. My mother looked everywhere but at my father, as if to do so would block her newfound freedom. My dad seemed preoccupied, maybe with plans he had after visiting me. We were an out-of-sync trio pulling off one last performance.

Still, sitting on my bed with them on either side of me, I had overwhelming gratitude.

Colang was actually two camps, a "brother" and "sister" camp, but we only mixed with the boys' camp once toward the end of the summer for the Fair. On that day, the entire playing field of the boys' camp was set up with game booths and food stands. I was playing one of the games, trying to throw a ball into a bull's-eye hole, when behind me I heard, "Here, let me show you how to hold your arm." His name was Mark Mandel, and he was ten too. He had a kind Pooh Bear face. We started walking around the Fair together. When we passed the mock marriage booth, Mark said, "Let's go in."

It was dark, and our eyes had to adjust from the sunlit day. A counselor put a tiara on my head that had a long organdy veil and handed me a bunch of flowers, saying, "Here's your bridal bouquet." Mark was given a tuxedo jacket and a bow tie.

We were sent farther back in the booth to the "Rabbi," a counselor wearing a black smock. We recited mock marriage vows, and Mark place a tinfoil ring on my left finger. I felt gushy inside, like the bottom of a lake.

I had to give back the tiara, but I got to keep the ring and a mock marriage certificate that Mark and I had each been given. It had fancy scroll-type writing that gave our names and the date and said we'd been joined in "mock matrimony." I wondered if my parents had a real marriage certificate. I'd never seen one in their red leather wedding album. It sat on our living room coffee table until my dad moved out. The album was a dark kind of red, and the cover had gold trimming that formed a box in which gold letters said, "Lucille & Ed, November 12, 1946."

It was years before I could read that. I started out rubbing and smelling the leather and having my mom turn the pages so I could look at the photographs. They were in black and white, but I'd imagine the colors of the flowers and the ladies' dresses.

My mother's hair looked darker and longer than I'd ever seen it. Her dress was white satin and glistened from its many folds. It went to the floor and then spilled behind her like puddles of milk. Her veil was sheer, like Tinker Bell's wings.

When I returned to school, I was in the sixth grade. I started saying that my parents were divorced. I hadn't planned to reveal it; my mouth just said it. I was relieved not to be keeping it a secret. I could have friends stay for sleepovers again without having to worry about explaining where my father was.

Some kids didn't react, and others asked me if I still got to see my dad. It wasn't the big deal to them I had feared it would be. They treated me the same as before.

Somehow, I had survived that first year of my parent's divorce—not that I was OK about it, that I ever would be. But I had learned already that life didn't care what I was or was not OK about; life happened, and I had to live with it. All I got to choose was how I did that.

The Voice

In the fall of 1990, I decided to treat myself to a vacation in the Bahamas the week before Christmas. I would be spending Christmas week with my mother in Boca Raton, Florida, so a week by myself on Paradise Island in Nassau was the perfect retreat. I had had a hard year.

At the start of 1990, the boyfriend I'd been with for over two years told me he was reconnecting with his former girlfriend, and we'd broken up quickly and, for me, painfully. Within a few months, they were engaged, then married.

I'd spent most of 1990 reflecting on what I had been doing with this man since he wasn't really for me and all my friends had kept telling me I was trying to fit a square peg in a round hole. I realized that I had felt desperate, and so had grabbed on to him, ready to settle for him rather than be alone any longer. By late 1990, I actually felt his former love had done me a huge favor by coming back around to claim him.

My week on Paradise Island was going to be just for me. Friends had suggested I go to the Club Med there because for meals I would be seated with people, and also there were lots of camp-like activities for me to enjoy if I chose, but other than this, I could have my own room by paying a little extra and have as much privacy and solitude as I wanted. Usually Club Med paired people in rooms to keep their costs down so that total strangers were very often roommates. I was happy to pay more to have my own accommodation. I arrived to gorgeous weather on a Saturday, and Club Med had a van to meet people at the airport. I befriended a few other guests in the van and sat with them at dinner. On Sunday, I met them and a few more people at the beach and had a lovely day in the sun. I was utterly happy to be on this beautiful island, and all was well in my world.

The meals were buffet and included in the vacation package. The procedure was that guests would first be shown to seats at tables for up to ten people. Then, they would go get trays and food. On Monday morning, my third day there, I got to breakfast around 9:00 a.m., and the hostess showed me to a table. I put my sweater on the chair and headed back to the buffet. Club Med was known for its fabulous meals. There were two huge buffet rooms loaded with every kind of hot and cold dish for every kind of taste bud. As I served myself some mixed fruit, a man positioned himself right next to me and put out his hand.

"Hi, my name is Rick," he said loudly and smiling. I immediately tightened, my New York City body ready to bolt. While I didn't actually carry Mace, I was always ready to ward off weirdos! That came with the urban turf. Also, I never wanted to lead a man on, be a tease. I knew that I was in no way attracted to Rick, so why encourage him? Simultaneously as I stiffened, in my left ear, I heard a voice so loud I all but turned to see who was talking. The voice spoke to me in a powerful, no-nonsense command, saying, "Be nice to him! You're not in New York! You don't have to marry him! Just be nice to him!" I was so startled; my hand shot out and shook his. I said my name was Joanne. He said he was from the Philadelphia area, and I said I was from New York City. He said he'd just arrived the day before. I nodded and then turned to go to another table of food. I wasn't at all sure what was happening. I returned to my seat and started eating. Within a few minutes, Rick showed up, having been assigned a seat across from mine. Boy, was he glad to see me, someone at the table he already knew. He grinned and started making more conversation. I once more had the reaction to be aloof and not encourage him. Yet again, in my left ear, I heard the voice: "Be nice to him! Talk to him! You don't have to marry him! Just be nice to him!" So, I loosened up and chatted with him and others at the table until breakfast was over. Then, I went to a golf lesson I had scheduled for myself.

Later, I went to lunch and then put on my bathing suit, with the plan to go sit on the beach and read my *New Yorker* magazine. It was about 2:00 p.m. on Monday, December 17. I was entering the beach from a set of wooden steps when I heard, "Joanne, hi there!" It was Rick, walking along in his bathing suit with another man. Even though I was not thrilled, I walked over to them. Rick introduced the other man, Alan, whom he had just met the day before when they had both arrived and been assigned to be roommates. This was their first day at the beach. Rick said, "Please join us," and Alan said, "Can I get you a chair?"

I looked at him and said, "A gentleman in our midst. How nice. Yes, please."

So we three got settled and looked at the sea, the small waves lapping the white sand, changing shades of blue and green. After about twenty minutes, Rick jumped up and said he was going to a sailing lesson and asked if we wanted to come. We declined. Now by ourselves, Alan and I started to get to know each other. He was separated for two years and had a daughter in high school. I was divorced from my second husband for six years and had a daughter in college. He was an accountant and lived in New Jersey, just over the George Washington Bridge in Leonia. I lived on the Upper East Side of Manhattan and worked in television. He seemed like a nice enough man, and I was enjoying talking to him, but that was all. Then, Alan said, "It's so hot. Would you like to go get a cold drink?" I looked at my watch and saw that it was almost four o'clock. I said, "Sure, but we'd better go now, because at five they play classical music outside, and I want to go hear it," and as I delivered this information to him, my private New York snob thought was, Not that this accountant from New Jersey would have any clue! He answered, "Oh yes, I know, and today they are playing Beethoven's Third Symphony!" That was the moment that felt like a lightning strike. I looked at him, almost disbelievingly and said, "You like Beethoven?" in a dreamy, soft voice I hardly knew, and it was mine!

He went on to talk all about his passion for classical music, theater, and art while we went and had our cold drink. Then, we parted long enough to change out of our bathing suits and meet at classical music. We sat next to each other in lawn chairs, a light, balmy breeze fanning us as the sun began to set. When the music started, he whispered in my ear that early Beethoven sounded like late Mozart. My eyes were closed as he said this. His voice poured right through my soul and claimed me to it. I wanted to hear it always.

We went to dinner and were seated at a big table as usual. People at it thought we were newlyweds on our honeymoon. We explained that actually, we'd just met.

The next day, we went into Nassau to walk around. Alan bought a leather briefcase in a store, and we just knew that the sales lady thought we were married. We understood that we seemed that way not only to others but also to each other.

We marveled at the instant connection we'd felt sitting on the beach just an hour after we'd met. We felt as if we'd known each other for years, and we felt a comfort that means family. We were also unabashedly smitten with each other. We were both in our forties and had had failed marriages, so even though we couldn't get enough of each other every day, Alan went back to his room each night while I slept alone in mine, pinching myself to see if I was dreaming or awake. While we did start kissing on the second day we knew each other, we decided not to take the romance any further than that until we were both back home in our real lives.

We spent our days and nights that week talking about anything and everything. We were inseparable until bedtime. On the day that I left to be with my mother in Florida, we exchanged phone numbers. By the time I was settled at my mother's condo, Alan was calling to make sure I'd arrived safely. He went home to New Jersey the next day, and we talked every night on the phone until I, too, got back a few days after Christmas. While I was still away, Alan informed the few women he'd been dating that he had met someone significant and would only be seeing her. I did not ask him to do this, but I, too, felt I did not want to date anyone else. We went out on New Year's Eve and started 1991 madly in love. Alan moved in with me that June. We married in August of 1993 and celebrated twenty wondrous years of marriage last summer. Over the years, we have thought of Rick and the part he unknowingly played in our fate. The voice demanding that I be nice to him was certainly spiritual and deep. I felt that then and whenever I recall that moment at the buffet. Rick had come to Nassau to gamble. He would get back to the room in the predawn poorer and a bit drunk well after Alan was asleep. We didn't spend time with Rick and never even got his last name or information, which we later on wished we had just so we could let him know we were together. We still put kind well wishes for Rick out into the universe now and then.

We celebrate both our wedding anniversary and December 17 each year. That date, we learned later on, is ironically Beethoven's birthday. It is also the day on which, when Alan and I least expected it, our lives were forever changed.

The Christmas Tree

When I was a small child growing up in New York City, I knew I was Jewish, but I thought just about everyone else was too. My family was, most of the kids at school seemed to be, and so I thought being a person meant being Jewish.

My mother and father were not observant, and we did not belong to a temple.

My mother's parents did, and sometimes we went to services on the High Holidays with them, so I knew about Rosh Hashanah and Yom Kippur. My maternal grandparents also had a Seder dinner at Passover, so I knew about that holiday too. For me, all of these holidays came once a year, just like Christmas. My mother wanted me to have Christmas. She wanted me to have the fantasy and joy of Santa Claus, toys, Rudolph pulling the flying sled, the whole deal. I don't know if she had it or not, but for sure, she wanted it for me, and so we always got a Christmas tree, which we decorated, with tinsel, angel hair, ornaments, lights, and a pretty star on top. I watched *Babes in Toyland* every year on TV and sang Christmas carols at school in chorus, where I was an alto. I liked Rosh Hashanah and Passover, but I loved Christmas. It was the holiday specifically for children. After all, Santa Claus didn't bring presents for the grown-ups! I went to sleep on Christmas Eve ready to burst with excitement. The year I was seven, I even dreamed I saw Santa in the living room of our eleventh-floor apartment with his bag! Waking up on Christmas morning, venturing out to the tree, seeing all the gifts wrapped and ready and my parents coming out of their room to see what Santa had brought was about as good as it got for me.

The fact that part of Christmas every year was the story of the baby Jesus, cradled in the manger with his parents and some other people, fit for me then.

After all, Christmas was for kids, so why wouldn't there be a little boy in there somewhere? I in no way knew or ever thought it was about religion any more than I thought being Jewish was about religion. It was just all a cohesive part of life for me for my first decade. At age ten, I learned about religious and ethnic differences. I was shocked to find out that Jewish people were a minority making up a tiny percentage of the world's population!

When I had my own daughter, I wanted her to have Christmas as well as the other holidays. Her father, my husband at the time, had had a Jewish father and a Christian mother and had also been raised having Christmas, so we got gorgeous live trees and decorated them each year. After we divorced, I still got a tree, and Santa still came. We also celebrated the High Holidays and made Seder.

At Christmas, my daughter and I would bake gingerbread cookies and make candy, and at Passover, we'd make haroseth and latkes! Of all the holidays we share, Christmas is still my favorite, and for me, as the song says, "It's the most wonderful time of the year!"

When I was forty-three and my daughter was twenty, I met the love of my life, Alan. Within months, he moved in, and we married two years later. Alan had been raised conservatively, going to shul, learning Hebrew, and having a bar mitzvah. We introduced our mothers to each other at the first Seder we made as a couple. We spent our first High Holidays together attending services at the Ninety-Second Street Y, where we still go twenty-three years later.

Alan and I met in the Bahamas one week before Christmas in 1990. I was there on vacation before going to Florida to spend Christmas with my mother.

That was our holiday more than any other, and for me it meant love, family, and joy.

Sadly, my mother passed away a few years after Alan and I met. So, by Christmas 1993, he and I were husband and wife, and my mom was gone. That year, we were in the Berkshires and had Christmas dinner at the Red Lion Inn with our daughters. For Alan, it was a first, and he went reluctantly, emphasizing that for him it was just a night out for dinner and nothing more. He had zero Christmas feelings and could not in any way relate to my Christmas feelings. He told me he absolutely could not and would not live with a Christmas tree; it would for him be completely wrong, a denouncement of his heritage and almost sacrilegious. His feelings were so strong that I felt I had no choice but to accept and respect them, and so once he and I made a home together, I no longer got my annual tree. All my decorations were still in a box but stored away and not used.

I tried to be OK about it, but I just wasn't. Every year by mid-December, I got so sad and melancholy, it was palpable. I insisted that we go see the tree at Rockefeller Plaza or that we go at least to a Christmas-type place for dinner on Christmas Eve. When my daughter was near, she and I would have some kind of celebration, and in her home, she'd have a tree, which I could enjoy while there. We lived on York Avenue, and every year the people who sold a variety of fresh-cut, pine-smelling trees would set up forests of them on our street and in our neighborhood so that wherever we were walking, I would longingly look at them, asking and eventually begging Alan to let me get even just a very small one. Always he vehemently answered no, upset that I would ask this of him. Finally, I gave up, but I could not, no matter how hard I tried, conceal my sadness each year. Sometimes, my eyes would overflow with tears I was trying not to shed. Sooner or later every December, I would have to just for the record tell him how deeply sad I was; I called it my "Christmas feelings" and left it at that, just wanting him to know it was not his fault, I did not blame or resent him for the way *he* felt; I totally understood and respected how he felt, but nevertheless I couldn't help the blues that came over me each year.

This went on for about sixteen years. Then, one evening in mid-December of 2007, I got to our apartment, put my key in the lock, and as I opened the door, I almost tripped over a beautiful small Fraser fir tree in a stand. Alan had bought it on his way home. I was stunned, surprised, and utterly overwhelmed with the enormous love and generosity of this gift. I started to cry and held him, and he started to cry. I told him, "This is it. You never, ever have to get me any other present. This is the most wonderful gift you could have ever given to me—you have showered me in diamonds with this tree!"

Part of what so touched me to my core was that it would have been enough if Alan had just said yes to me and let me go buy a tree. The fact that this conservative Jewish man stood on the street amid all the trees, picked one out, bought it, carried it to our building, then walked it through the lobby and got on the elevator with it for anyone to see astounded me. It was such an act of love. He told me he could not go one more season seeing me so sad. After I thanked him profusely for quite a while, I delicately asked him if it would be all right if I decorated the tree in some fashion. He said it would be, but please no lights. I said fine, and the very next day I went and got decorations because my own box was in storage! Sitting on the floor that night and putting all the ornaments on my tree gave me incredible joy, and Alan was very happy for me.

I did not involve him at all in decorating the tree or even gazing at it with me. Getting it for me had been all he could do, given how he was raised. I in no way took that for granted. I told him that he was done; he had gone beyond what I ever would have imagined. The following year, I asked him if I could go out and get myself a tree. He said, "Yes, but please make it a small one."

And so, each year I have a very special date with myself to go get my tree. The sublime pleasure I experience doing so is unique to how I feel at and about Christmas. Each year I arrange to decorate my tree when Alan is out.

I blast Christmas music on the radio while placing each ornament just so until my tree takes my breath away.

When Alan comes home, I get to profusely thank him, yet again, for not only buying me that first tree but for living with one each Christmas since.

No Longer a Child of Divorce

Today, March 5, 2011 is my birthday. I am sixty-three years and five months old today. Even so, I feel newly born, emerged, and fresh, ready to log time.

Since I was nine and my parents divorced, I have had the burdensome backpack of self-blame to carry each and every step of the way. Somehow I imposed this on myself. My parents certainly did not say or even think the failure of their marriage was my fault. That didn't matter. The breakup of our family unit was an earthquake of colossal magnitude for me and broke me apart inside, both from the devastating loss and the visceral knowledge that somehow I was to blame. This was not a thought in my head at the time, just physical knowledge in my being, like breathing. My parents' divorce was confirmation of my biggest fear, that I was not wanted or valued, that I wasn't worth them staying together.

Feeling that way meant I had to compensate, big time. I had to accommodate, please everyone, "make things OK" from waking to sleeping. I mastered these behaviors both personally and professionally. Only as I perceived approval coming my way could I relax and feel safe. Still, I didn't feel I was "enough." Had I been "enough" for my parents, for their marriage?

I have not gone from über–people pleaser to proclaiming my "birthday" today over night. I have been shedding the need to please, the need for approval from others for some time now. It has been a process of getting older, wiser, and mercifully more comfortable in my own skin. It is definitely well worth aging for.

Still, with my father, all bets have been off. With him, I still have needed approval, and I have never felt I was enough.

Only now, this week, after a visit to California to celebrate my father's ninetieth birthday, have I finally "gotten it" in my bones that the divorce was never about me. My father was meant to meet Ellen when I was in my early twenties and marry and be happy with her coming up on forty years. My mother was meant to continue to evolve within herself and to try also to have that romantic partnership that sadly eluded her. She passed away in 1992.

My visit to California was something I had to do for myself. I wanted to be with my father as he turned ninety. I had not needed to be with him for a whole host of prior birthdays, including eighty and eighty-five. His main family life was with Ellen and her two daughters and the four grandchildren her daughters had produced.

Since 1970, my father and I have lived on opposite coasts. First, he in New York and I in California, and then ironically, in 1984, when I finally moved back east, he and Ellen moved to the Bay Area because that's where her daughters were living, among other reasons.

Ellen and I had gone through a period of several years where we hadn't spoken to each other, and this had put a strain on my relationship with my dad. It was over money I had inherited from my mother's father that Ellen felt entitled to. My father didn't feel that way, but he knew better than to go against his wife.

By the time I was heading to California, however, Ellen and I were on speaking terms, although not much more than that. I do not like to fly, and this was one reason I had not made it out to California to see the new home in Santa Rosa they'd been in for three years. Whenever they had come east, I had spent time with them, had even been instrumental in bringing them to New York, paying their airfare and hotel so I could see my dad without having to get on an airplane.

Once I'd decided to be with him for his ninetieth birthday, I knew I would get to him by train. I love train rides and had researched a number of times the trip from New York to the San Francisco area, so I knew what to do. I'm sure my dad and Ellen thought I was nuts to spend three nights each way on a train, but for me it was extremely enjoyable and gave me time going and then returning home to digest being with them on their turf. It was on the train ride home that I realized, in a flash of enlightenment, that my parents' divorce had not, in any way, ever been my fault. That moment alone was worth all the train time! It came to me late at night, as I lay in my bed in my tiny train compartment. I think we were somewhere in Nebraska, heading toward Chicago, where I would get off and get on another train to New York City. I had been thinking, reliving really, the days I had just spent in Santa Rosa with my dad and Ellen, listening to a pretty nonstop dialogue of their lives there, the wines they had tasted, the restaurants they loved, the movies, operas, and ballets they'd attended. Not one time had Ellen asked about Eve, mentioned her name, even though Eve is my daughter's child and my father's only great-grandchild. Nor had she or my dad asked about my daughter, Judy, or my husband, Alan. Their entire conversation revolved around themselves.

I had one lunch alone with my dad during the trip, and as the waitress cleared our plates, he turned to me with watery ninety-year-old eyes and said, "Tell me about the baby." Eve had just turned four. I brought out my camera for the first time since I'd arrived and showed him a bunch of adorable pictures, which he seemed to thoroughly enjoy.

Except for that lunch, my visit was with and about them and Ellen's daughters and their lives and those of their grown children. We had an elegant and expensive dinner in my dad's honor at a fabulous restaurant in San Francisco, and while I had been having a mix of feelings being with them all during that week, by the birthday dinner I was utterly thrilled to be there.

I got on the train home feeling the mission had been accomplished. I was glad to be going home, to my people and my life. I realized that my dad's people—his life was there with them and had been for decades. Yes, we kept in touch by phone, had good and sometimes close talks and infrequent visits, but really he was Ellen's husband, her daughters' stepdad, and their children's grandfather, and—here's where the lightning strike comes in—none of it was my fault! He wasn't supposed to spend his life married to my mom. It was his life, period, not about me—just about him and his life and what worked for him, and that was all, finished, no one's fault or responsibility to fix, take care of, be enough for, be pleasing to, etc., etc., etc. It was late at night on the train when I realized this deeply, as deep as I go.

I was glad to be alone in my berth because I started to sob pretty uncontrollably as I kept saying, "It wasn't my fault" to myself. It was the first time I had ever felt those words to be true.

And as I have now come to realize, it was never about me being enough for my dad. I was always enough for him just by being me. He loved me in his own self-propelled way, which did not include making me the priority in his life. It's my birthday today because I understand that this is about him, not my unworthiness of being his priority. He has been the best dad he could be given who he is, not given who I am.

Being a Grandma

Being a grandma is not for every woman. Some do not even want to be called "Grandma." These women cringe at that word, which for them is equivalent to "old," which for them is something negative. I am not one of these women. For me, being a grandma is a greatly fulfilling blessing.

I am fortunate to be able to be a hands-on grandma. I have one daughter, Judy, and she has one daughter, Eve. They live close by, and my daughter works from home on a schedule that has permitted her to be a mother first and foremost, which was what she wanted very much. Having me available to help out as needed worked well for her but even better for me. Every time she thanks me profusely for coming to cover for her, sometimes with only a day's notice, I in turn thank her in spades.

There are a myriad of reasons why I so love being a grandma. Most importantly, I get to spend meaningful time with Judy and Eve. Having had two loving and devoted grandmothers myself until I was twenty-one and one passed away, I know as deep as I go what having grandmas is all about! My own mother and daughter had a very close bond until my mother passed away, when my daughter was in college. I was her only child and my daughter her only grandchild. Both my daughter and I were with my mother when she died.

My granddaughter knows that she owns me in a way that I knew I owned my grandmothers. I could not do anything to stop their love. They did at moments get cross with me or scold me for some behavior that was really annoying, but I knew even then that they loved me just as much as always. I felt incapable of being unlovable to my grandmothers. Only when I became a grandmother did I fully understand how they felt about me. It stunned me to realize how much I had meant to them from this new perspective. I am so grateful to be having the experience now for myself.

I have always kept the child I was alive and accessible inside. Because of this, I can sit on the floor for hours and play dolls with Eve and never get bored.

The total imagination I had as a small child comes right back as we make up our stories and use whatever we have available to embellish them. Even a piece of tissue or a paper clip can transform into a dress or a wand. What I enjoy when playing with Eve is the limitless world of fancy that has no lanes or barriers.

Everything is possible; plots twist, turn, and just become whatever we say they are.

This feels very freeing and good because it reminds me that I probably put more limits in my own way and life than are truly there. The current cliché "Think outside the box" comes to mind. Whenever I try to do this in my own life, I feel an expansion of possibilities.

Another thing I love about being a grandma is feeling my age, wisdom, and antiquity next to my granddaughter, who is now six and a half years old and in first grade. She is a brand-new person on this planet, just as I was at age six back in 1953. What a different world it is now. When I tell her there were no cell phones or computers when I was her age, she looks right past me with her lack of comprehension. I feel my years on this planet when I am next to her. I feel my oldness next to her youngness, and it feels good, meaty, and solid to me. I know she can feel it, too, in her own juvenile way. I felt it with my grandmas. I didn't think about it; it was just a sense I had. Being with them felt safe and steady, like being with a big tree that had lived a long time and weathered storms, sun, wind, and season upon season.

Recently I was babysitting Eve on a school night. I put her to bed and lay in the dark with her, telling her a story I was making up as I was going along. When I finished the story, she asked if I would sing to her. She does this when we have sleepovers too. I launched into a repertoire of Broadway show tunes and didn't stop singing for at least twenty minutes, even though I felt her nod off within ten.

I wanted to make sure she was fast asleep. As I sang, I got teary-eyed thinking that only she would want to hear my sixty-six-year-old, croaky-voiced a capella singing!

Part II

9/11 Journal (2001–16)

Sunday, 9/16/01, 4:30 p.m.

I bought this notebook yesterday, but I couldn't write in it. It is solely for my own words about the horror that occurred here in New York City on Tuesday, September 11, 2001.

My own account starts that morning at 8:40 a.m. or so, when I boarded the Eighty-Sixth Street crosstown bus at Ninety-First Street and York Avenue along with the usual number of morning commuters. I took the seat I usually do. (I am definitely a creature of habit where possible). As part of my daily routine, I put on my radio set at 880 News and listened into the headset while I put on my makeup. The bus next stopped at Eighty-Sixth Street and York. I finished my makeup. As we pulled into the stop at Eighty-Sixth Street and First Avenue, it was 8:48 a.m., time for the traffic and weather report. Instead of talking about the traffic, the reporter in the helicopter informed the anchors that there was a lot of smoke coming from one of the towers at the World Trade Center and that a fire was also raging. Then he commented that there seemed to be a hole, "as if something went into the tower." At this point, the anchor cut in with breaking news that apparently a commuter plane had crashed into a tower at the World Trade Center. They even had a young lady on the phone who called in to say she could see a "small plane" had flown too low and gone into the tower. By now, my bus was at Madison Avenue. I heard the bus driver's intercom dispatcher alerting all drivers to avoid the World Trade Center area. I pulled out my cell phone and called my office because I wanted to make sure they knew about this breaking news story that would probably preempt our live-at-nine television broadcast. It was 8:55 a.m. I reached someone who said yes, they were aware of an accident at the World Trade Center. I felt badly for whoever was on the plane and also feared for those whose offices were hit. It sounded like a freakish accident, a misjudgment perhaps by an inexperienced pilot. The towers are so much taller than anything around there, I thought; they're certainly hard to miss visually, so how did that poor plane get so close it couldn't veer off, even at the last minute? By now, my bus was going through the Eighty-Fifth Street transverse. It was 9:00 a.m. Suddenly, while still reporting the accident on the radio, the anchor starting yelling in disbelief, saying, "What, oh no, oh my God, another plane has crashed into the other tower—oh my God, another plane, a second plane, has gone into the other tower!"

And right then, I knew. I knew something was fucked-up—wrong—inexplicable by any means I had available in my fifty-three years and eleven months of life!

My body tensed up with the fear it still holds today. My bus came to its stop at Central Park West and Eighty-Sixth Street. I jumped off, shaking, and went to a pay phone because my cell wasn't getting me through to my daughter Judy's line. I got her machine and left an urgent message for her to call me because I was hearing on the radio all kinds of terrible trouble at the World Trade Center, where she sometimes goes on jogs or walks from her apartment on Ninth Street and Fifth Avenue. I was frantic to hear that she was OK and hadn't gone there right then. I boarded a bus going down Central Park West. I knew I wasn't getting on a subway because I felt too scared, and it seemed unsavory to go underground at that moment. As I got on, the bus driver, seeing my headset on, said, "Hey, you have a radio—what's going on at the World Trade Center?" I told him two planes had crashed into the towers and that it sounded deliberate, like terrorism, even though it felt surreally impossible that that could be. I even apologized for saying it sounded like terrorism because I didn't want to accuse someone unjustly—but it was too scary and suspect and not seeming accidental anymore.

As soon as I got to my office, I called Judy again and got her on the phone. I was so thankful she was safe, but also I was terribly upset, and she tried to calm me down, God bless her. We hung up, but then the president came on television and said it was an apparent terrorist attack. Then the Pentagon got hit, and I called Judy back to emphasize how very serious this was, terrifyingly so, and set up to stay in contact with her. She promised to stay at home. I then spoke with my stepdaughter, Lauren, who called from her work, freaked, and said she was coming up to my office to go home with me. Her boyfriend, Ken, works in New Jersey. Her dad, my husband, Alan, was also in New Jersey that day as it happened. (His office is in New York.) I had already called the New York office to get a message to him, if possible, in New Jersey. I was concerned and wanted to hear from him. I left my office with a few others and met Lauren, and we all went in one coworker's car to the East Side.

It took much longer because we had to drive up Central Park West to 110th Street because the transverses were closed. We had the radio on in the car as we drove and listened to the moment-to-moment updates on the unfolding story, still in disbelief.

Lauren and I stayed together while Alan and Ken were stuck overnight in New Jersey because almost immediately, all bridges, tunnels, and entries into Manhattan were shut down. Lauren and I tried to give blood at a few local hospitals, but they needed type O that was not ours. We stayed together at my and Alan's apartment.

He stayed in New Jersey, as did Lauren's boyfriend, Ken. Judy stayed at her home. It was a terrifying day and night, and yet we were also in shock. It seemed unreal.

9/21/01

Words don't come. When they do, they seem like fragments of something broken into countless pieces flying in all directions, irreconcilable, words like *pain, grief, sadness, horror, fury, rage, why?*

I will never, ever understand the cruelty shown yet again, this time here in New York City and Washington. It is beyond my comprehension that human beings can treat other human beings so inhumanely. These terrorists were infants once; we all were. The cold-blooded, calculated, complete disregard for innocent human beings—men, women, children—is beyond any understanding. Why can't people be kind? What is so hard, so unnatural about it? To me, being kind seems natural, pleasurable, and being cruel is something I only feel like being when I'm hurting. Are people hurting so very badly that they can be so unaccountably cruel? I hurt when I even want to be cruel, and I feel terrible if I actually say or do something cruel—an insult or sarcastic dig to someone I love.

The unspeakable cruelty that was shown in this terrorist attack, the utter disregard for life, is an evil that has shown itself in history, like a recurring nightmare that awakens one in terror.

The fact that a belief system, a set of ideas, of words put together in a particular way, can motivate human beings to such disgusting, despicable treatment of other living people—cutting off lives like slicing bread!

10/28/01

Now there's the treat of anthrax. It's showing up in letters, so ordinary mail is scary. It has to be examined, handled with caution, left unopened.

We are at war; we've been bombing Afghanistan since 10/7, and so far the Taliban are intact. We are straining the patience of our Arab allies and probably some of our European ones, even though they at least understand this war on terrorism will take a long time, maybe lifetimes.

Waking up each day since September 11 is

11/18/01

I got cut off above—never got back to the journal that day about what "waking up" was like. I think that day (10/28) I would have said waking up was still pretty terrifying. Today, I wouldn't say that exactly. It is still scary—I'm definitely on edge underneath everything a lot of the time—but I had a really good talk on the phone with my dad about two weeks ago. He told me not to let fear get the better of me—that if I did, they'd won. This calmed me down a bit, and I found and continue to find I have a certain resolve now, even with the fear, that I won't let them run me out of town, or win, period.

It has also been encouraging that in the past week, the war on terrorism has effectively driven the Taliban out of most of their holdings in Afghanistan. We, along with allies and the Northern Alliance, have been finally achieving some of our goals. This is still far from over, but at least we're gaining.

The lives lost and families affected by 9/11 are still very much a part of a collective sadness that lingers here and that Bob Herbert poignantly described recently in the *New York Times*.

I am getting along and on with my life, as are many, but I feel incredibly different deep down as I go about the same schedule and tasks and cover the same ground outwardly that I usually do in the course of my day. It's all the same, and it's all changed every moment because while I'm doing whatever I'm doing, even thinking whatever I'm thinking and saying whatever I'm saying, it's there, in me, part of me all the time: the images of the towers on fire; the unremitting billows of black, deadly smoke; the knowledge that people jumped; thoughts of sweet Thomas McHale, my dear friend Taryn's young husband, doomed almost immediately in Tower One at Cantor Fitzgerald, his firm. Tom had left for work as usual that morning, left his seven-months-pregnant wife (carrying their first child, a son), and he had no inkling what was going to happen to him within a few hours.

I look at babies in strollers so sweet, uncomprehending of the world that now is theirs, a world very different—at least in America—than the one my daughter and I have grown up in. Maybe for these babies, an America guarded by visible, palpable security measures will be no big deal, the status quo for them—what they've always known. Maybe it's hardest for us now, who have lost an America we used to have.

12/25/01

Christmas morning 2001, a year no one saw coming. Everyone was worried about 2000, the new millennium. Two thousand was the unknown, so when 2000 came and went pretty smoothly, we all relaxed. We were all well into 2001, another smooth second year in the new millennium mode. But nine months, eleven days into that new year, the time it takes for a baby to be conceived and born, the horrific, unspeakable terrorist attacks brought Americans up short, and we pulled together and fought back, are still doing so. Being an American is again a passionately prideful claim. Our differences in this country still exist and must continue to be addressed, but our collective American identity has empowered us and given us spirited hope in a disturbing, scary, and troubled time in our history. We are the target for a hateful group of human beings who use themselves, their own flesh, as weapons.

It is still almost inconceivable to me that actual human beings can treat one another so evilly, and yet I am more than sobered by not only the reality of 9/11 here but by the countless, never-ending examples throughout the history of this earth. Since time on earth by humans has been recorded, human beings have committed heartless, barbaric acts of murder, torture, and cruelty on other humans.

Innocent people, women, children, and the elderly, as well as men, have been slaughtered. The immoral disregard for human life, for life given by a power greater than any human's (no matter what name one calls the power by), continues to shock and infuriate me even though it is all too familiar.

Again, I say these people were once innocent babies sucking the breast or bottle—were they born so hateful, so disrespectful of their species? Does the instinct to survive include a component need to destroy others who seem different because of their beliefs or appearance or whatever, even though they are also human beings?

The terrorists' twisted notion of a "holy war" is one example of how an ideology can justify the murder of completely innocent beings of all types, indiscriminately, like the Nazis murdered Jews for being Jews.

We have responded to the attack by entering a war on terrorism. In that pursuit, we, too, have had civilian casualties—unintentional at least, collateral damage we try to minimize while needing to respond to the terrorist threat.

Still, I wish that all human beings on this earth would respond to an even higher, more emphatic moral and ethical creed to not shed human blood, to respect life, the G-d-given gift that must not be taken for granted so heinously.

I know this statement is lofty, completely unrealistic, and idealistic. It's not even the way the laws of nature operate. Stronger overcomes weaker, animals, insects, birds, reptiles—all living things do destroy other living things for survival. Perhaps we are experiencing the human version of survival, a mutant strain of which is the kind of evil that has been displayed over time. Is that the element that made the Jews the object of Nazi ideology and Americans the object of extreme Islamic terrorists?

Christmas is a time for love, peace, compassion, and, if possible, forgiveness.

I must admit I don't feel particularly forgiving this year. The images from 9/11 are still with me, enraging me, devastating me, making me want those who caused it to be obliterated.

8/3/02

Many months have passed since I wrote in this journal. Two thousand two has been passing and its one main distinction for me is that it's not 2001. The new year at least made me feel a slight shift of movement, of next, of turning one corner in the healing but only a small, albeit valued, shift.

I at least got calmer, finally, after pretty much being in a "freaked-out" state from 9/11 until the new year. Somehow, I let go of some of that tension; I still can scare extremely easily, but I'm not tensed up all the time, even when I sleep, the way I was. I have not taken a subway—just haven't needed to. I would if I had to but only then. I have absolutely no desire to fly—I never have liked it and have only flown when it was necessary. Now, I want even less to get on a plane.

We took the train to Florida in January. I was scared but resolved to not let the terrorist threat stop me from living life as I would normally do.

My friend Taryn is doing admirably given her circumstances. She gave birth to Collin Thomas McHale on 10/18/01—he's a beautiful, sweet boy with a lot of his father, Tom, in him, a father he will only know by the memories of others, photos, maybe some video.

The people who lost loved ones on 9/11 have an immensely sad bond.

The world, to me, seems in a dark and dangerous place. Threats of terrorism of all kinds continue and are painfully real now to Americans, who have joined the club, so to speak, of humans on this globe dealing with this kind of threat.

While I support President Bush and our government to do what must be done to protect Americans, I also sense and fear the motives and agendas of some of their decisions. Politics seems never to be forgotten, ignored, or even put on a back burner. I fear a certain near evil agenda that could also be coming from our own leaders when their personal power is threatened.

9/10/02

It is Tuesday, September 10, and for at least a week the images and memories of 9/11/01 have come again as the first anniversary of the terror attacks is here.

The TV shows are endless: recaps; documentaries; victims' relatives' stories; survivors' stories; police, fire department, and port authority stories; World Trade Center builders' stories; nonending replays of the towers burning, collapsing. It's a TV show, and because of all the media replays, edits, sound bites, isos, shots, cuts, close-ups, pullouts, dissolves, pull-ins—it desensitizes in a certain way. It's a movie, not real life in real time where there was horror, confusion, terror, pain, pulverization, suicide leaps out of windows, smoke-inhalation pass-outs, bodies crushed, exploded, burned happening in real, unedited time from 8:46 a.m. until 10:28 a.m. and thereafter for some few survivors in the rubble who made it out or others at hospitals. One lady is still in a hospital.

The real horror—the real history to be recorded and not forgotten is the swift time—102 minutes—that changed so much—during which so many were lost here in New York. Also the real time of those four flights and the tragic souls trapped in those planes, unedited, doomed.

I work in TV—have made my own career in TV—I understand what TV is about, how it works, how shows are put together. I understand the medium; I respect it in certain ways, but I just got too desensitized watching the neatly formatted programs—as good as they were in some ways.

9/11 is just too overwhelming for "format."

9/11/06

Today the networks all competed to have the best, most-watched fifth-anniversary coverage. The ceremony at ground zero was touching and sincere, with moments of silence at 8:46 a.m., 9:03 a.m., 9:59 a.m., and 10:29 a.m. The families of the victims reading the names was also very moving. Five years later, those who perished have in no way been forgotten by the people to whom they mattered.

I could relate and feel for the family members—the real people on television as they remembered their loved ones—but many (not all) of the on-air people—hosts, interviewers—seemed to be so manufactured, given time cues and prompters and keeping the programs at clipped paces. One on-air person said, "We're getting a wrap," as if that were more important than what was being remembered by the guest being interviewed—very crass, very about sound bites, and not particularly compassionate.

The worst was yet to come, when, at 9:00 p.m., the president gave an outrageous seventeen-minute speech to the country. It revolted me—was the most manipulative, slick, cheap shot, scam, spin piece of garbage with consummate audacity in every sentence. He actually played the American people on this anniversary—actually had the gall to use the occasion for his own political agenda, which includes trying to have a legacy of justification for his invasion of Iraq. History, in my opinion, will not provide this legacy no matter how many speeches Cheney writes for him!

It was so appalling to watch and listen to this—I did it on purpose to see just how despicable he could be on such a solemn, sad day of remembrance. I wonder how people can watch and listen to his words and not feel had, big time.

What a sad state our country is in. The people that make up the American population are so much better, I believe, than the handful that runs it.

I am sad today and also somewhat numb—the overwhelming hugeness of the September 11, 2001, terrorist attacks is never diminished.

9/11/11, Tenth Anniversary—Evening

I have just reread this entire journal. I had not done so for many years. After that fifth anniversary, which is the entry before this, I think I just felt the solemnness of the ensuing anniversaries as I went about the day, but I did not need to write in this journal.

I am much calmer than I was initially. The altered, surreal state of the real, undeniable threat of terrorism has over these ten years become the norm. Heightened security, measures taken both publicly and privately, flying, showing photo ID entering most large buildings—so many details have become routine. Life feels normal within this new norm. Actually, it was "new" several years ago, the result of the 9/11 terrorist attack—which as I refer to it right now feels like a normal matter-of-fact event that happened, a historical one that still saddens me deeply but does not cause me to shake the way I described it had when it occurred.

Today was a defining anniversary in that the 9/11 Memorial at ground zero opened and the building of two Freedom Towers is well under way. The first is close to completion, and a second one will be built as well. Sadly and revealingly, I don't know all of the specific plans—I have in the past few years distanced myself some from the tragic, raw pain that is and always will be when recalled: 9/11/01. I have not forgotten—no one ever will—but I have moved on in many meaningful ways on my own personal journey, and this has been my focus.

One beautiful and, I think, very and utterly appropriate part of the memorial is the creation of the two "footsteps" right where the two towers stood. Too hard to describe here—each has a shelf of water spilling along its wall—water that is life-giving and renewing, and the water is funneled down a hole in the middle of each footprint in remembrance of those who were lost.

Some of the children who lost a parent on that day chose to talk today during the memorial, and their words were heartbreaking and also very life-affirming. Many said they spent each day trying to do and be what would have made their parent—usually a father—proud. Three sons of a fireman who left six children behind are becoming firemen like their beloved and so missed father.

The real story today of 9/11/01 these ten years later is that thousands upon thousands of wives, fathers, mothers, husbands, sons, daughters, sisters, brothers, grandparents, friends, and coworkers have not in any way forgotten their loved ones—so many have shown inspirational love, dignity, grace, bravery, and fortitude in dealing with their losses.

Sadly, the unity of America that I described as one aspect of 9/11/01—that patriotic we-are-all-one-people mind-set—is completely gone now in 2011.

The country is more divided than before 9/11 occurred. There are some scary, extreme ideologies being worked into our mainstream, and the political state of affairs is not encouraging.

Money rules, power seems about money, greed is back, and true moral and ethical values are so nonexistent that I sound fanciful even alluding to them! Ten years ago, when I started this journal, I would not have believed or imagined the state of divisiveness we are currently experiencing. But I also would not have imagined that just seven years later we would elect our first black president, so maybe now is backlash for that, which was a remarkable and to my mind wonderful event in our history. I was very proud of our country then but am concerned about it now.

I got offtrack just now.

Back to 9/11/11—this tenth anniversary. Just four months ago, our Navy SEALs found and killed the head perpetrator of the 9/11/01 attacks. I refuse to write that name in this journal. I was glad if it gave any closure to those who lost loved ones. Also, just a few days ago, we were informed about a credible, specific, but not confirmed terror threat to New York and/or Washington,

DC, on or around this tenth anniversary. This has triggered some fear again, but I will not let it stop me from doing my life just like everyone else. Most people, if not all—New Yorkers anyhow—have said as much, and I agree with them.

9/11/14, Thirteenth Anniversary of 9/11

I now live in New Jersey. I miss living in New York City and hope to again, if it is meant to happen. I was aware of the 9/11 anniversary this week in a sad, calm way.

Thirteen years is quite some time. Collin Thomas McHale turns thirteen next month, and his mom, Taryn, is married to a wonderful "alive dad" for Collin, and there is a sister/daughter, Riley, who is seven. When Taryn married Dan, Collin was five. He said, "Now I have two dads—one in heaven and one on earth."

Life has gone on as it always does, as it must. We now have a terror threat from another radical group in the Middle East, called ISIS. Just last night, President Obama (who got reelected in 2012) spoke to the nation about actions the United States will take against this terrorist group. I went about the day aware of the anniversary, sad about it, but not really observing it. I went to a spin class at 8:45 a.m. and then to a weights class at 9:30 a.m. So I was not observing the moments of silence outwardly, but inwardly, I was aware of the time, of what it meant. I have been aware all day of this day, have said prayers in my thoughts to Tom McHale and all of the souls who were lost that horrible day. To recall that day *any* time is to relive its devastating horror. That doesn't ever go away.

9/11/15, Fourteenth Anniversary of 9/11

As I write this, I am hearing names of those lost, which are read every year on this anniversary date. Ironically, I just heard Thomas McHale's name read; I had not been listening for the past hour, had been watching a rebroadcast of NBC's *Today Show* on the actual date, 9/11/01.

Fourteen years later, for me, means I can watch or listen to accounts of that day with some distance from the trauma felt at the time. I listened more than watched. I found it still hard to look at the two buildings struck and burning and then horrifically collapsing. But I did, at moments, force myself to look, to say to myself that I am a witness. I was a fifty-three-year-old woman then who experienced this as a New Yorker, as one whose dear friend Taryn—seven months pregnant with her and her husband Tom McHale's first child, a son—lost her beloved husband. I am utterly thankful for her life now and the good life that son Collin is living.

As these names are being read, by family and friends of those lost, it is heartening to know that life, even after the most devastating losses, does go on. The living remember. That is the key; that is why I made myself look, so as to never forget.

9/11/16, Fifteenth Anniversary of 9/11

It is Sunday evening, and I just came inside from our terrace. I had gone out to see the two beams of light that are visible from ground zero on the anniversary each year. Light is hope, and given the magnitude of the tragedy that was, is, and will always be September 11, 2001, the beams of light are a remembrance of loss and also, I feel, the hope that has also been part of these past fifteen years.

The hope that this will never, ever happen again. The hope that is part of life and the living who were able to survive on that day, get out of the buildings before they fell. Many of those people got out because of the help of a first responder.

Today I went to a 9/11 remembrance ceremony at Constitution Park in Fort Lee, New Jersey, where I live. They have two pieces of wreckage, one from each building, as a monument of remembrance. A lady spoke who had been helped out of one of the buildings by a first responder. It was very moving. I spoke with her briefly afterward. She said that for her, there was before 9/11 and then after.

Part III

Fiction (1983–2019)

Loving Fenton

It was 1970, a brand-new decade, and Hilary was in love. It happened so quickly, so effortlessly, that she was feeling silly and unlike anyone she knew. Fenton was her boyfriend of only three weeks, but already he was talking to her about "the rest of our lives." He was a little older than she, thirty to her twenty-five. Hilary had met Fenton at a cocktail party. He was holding a martini, standing apart from others, and as her eyes grazed his, he smiled and gave the slightest "come here" nod. They introduced themselves and talked for a while. When the party broke up, he suggested they have dinner. By the time the meal was over, she felt like she'd know him half her life. He was easy to talk to and fully listened to what she had to say. He was an associate attorney at a medium-sized law firm and hoped to eventually make partner. He thought her job, as a teacher, was neat because of all the time off she got.

"The thing about law school and then work in a law firm is forget having much time off until retirement," he said that first night.

"Well, I do like my teaching schedule, but that's not why I went into it. I love kids and wanted to help them learn," Hilary said pointedly.

They went out on a few more dates before they made love at Hilary's apartment. Fenton stayed the night but had to leave for an early morning meeting even though it was Saturday. A client was in town from somewhere for the weekend. Hilary had gotten up and made coffee for them before he left. Sitting alone at her tiny table by the window after he'd gone, sipping her now cold coffee, she thought about their night together. Kissing Fenton was wonderful, the best she could remember. He'd held her for a long time after he climaxed. Then he'd gotten up to use the bathroom, and she had turned over and settled into her pillow feeling warm and safe.

They seamlessly began life as a couple. He mostly stayed with her, but she also spent nights with him in his studio apartment. They exchanged keys, so both homes felt like theirs. Hilary wished her mother were still living so she could tell her about Fenton. She'd never known her father, who had died when she was almost three.

She was an only child, so there were no siblings with whom to share her news. She did call her best friend, Ida, who lived in Florida. She and Ida had met in college, and Ida was also a teacher.

"I'm so happy for you, Hil," Ida had cooed upon hearing about Fenton.

"Well, we'll see what happens; it's still so new," Hilary replied. "I wish you were here so you could meet him."

"Yeah, me too. Maybe this summer I'll come up and meet him if you're still dating."

By summer Ida did come up but not just to meet Fenton. She was an attendee at Hilary and Fenton's wedding. They had hastily planned the small affair just four months after they'd met. Ida had even asked Hilary if she was expecting.

"Nope, although we do want a family some time sooner than later. But first we want to enjoy being married. It's been so fast, and yet it feels like it's been years."

The reason for their rush in marrying was due to Fenton's transfer from the East Coast office to the West Coast one. Fenton had been tapped to take a position in Los Angeles that moved him much closer to making partner. The dilemma for him was leaving Hilary in New York.

"But if you are my wife, they have to move us both," he'd said. "You can get a job out there, or just play during the day while I work. I'm getting a decent raise in pay, and I hear it's less expensive to live out there."

"No, I still want to teach or tutor or something like that," she'd said. He then reached into his pocket and presented her with a black velvet box that contained a lovely diamond that fit her finger with a tight hug.

"I want nothing so much as to be your wife," she said, shocked to realize how true her words were. Before meeting Fenton, marriage had seemed like some way-in-the-future event that would probably happen to her as she closed in on thirty. The previous boyfriends she'd had were fun or interesting or not, but none was memorable. She'd had a crush on a boy in high school, but he viewed her as a study buddy. At the time, she thought she was in love and felt down about his lack of interest. That was the only other time she'd even used the term "in love" in her head. Fenton had come into her life so unexpectedly, like in a fairy tale. He, too, was an only child, and although his parents were still living, he had not had contact with them for several years. When she asked why, he said that they had him late in their lives and that once he got into high school, they began traveling, what they called "taking back the time" he had cost them.

"I think maybe I was an accident. Maybe my parents just wanted to be with each other, but then there I was. That's a lot how I felt anyhow growing up. I had to work and save to go to college and law school. They were done when I turned eighteen," Fenton told her. Hilary had taken his hand and said, "Well, it's their loss for damn sure."

The fact that he had picked out a beautiful ring just for her touched her deeply. She was thrilled to be starting an exciting new chapter in her life, marrying and moving to sunny Los Angeles. She loved Fenton beyond what she'd imagined being in love would feel like. She was breaking so much new ground within herself and enjoying every second of it.

When the day arrived for their move out West, Fenton's good friend Bob Carter and his wife, Marlene, drove the newlyweds to JFK for their flight. Bob worked in the New York office, and he was happy for Fenton but still sad to be losing his work friend.

"We will just have to talk a lot on the company WATS line," Bob said at the gate. "We'll figure it out with that three-hour time difference. Marlene will check in with Hilary, too, see how it's going." They had all hugged one another, and Hilary was glad friends had seen them off. She liked Marlene although didn't know her that well. The two couples had been out for dinner a few times, and Bob and Marlene had been at the wedding, but now they were leaving and Hilary would have to make new friends. She wasn't great at that. She'd always been a bit solitary and content to be so. She hadn't been particularly popular at school or unpopular. She'd just been in the herd, going to classes, recess, lunch, and home. Sometimes she'd have a girl over for a visit or to study with, but only Ida had garnered best friend status with her.

Fenton's firm had a furnished apartment in Westwood that he and Hilary lived in their first month while looking for their own home. Since Fenton had to hit the ground and run at the office, Hilary's job was to apartment hunt, check out neighborhoods, and then line up possible places for Fenton to see on the weekend.

Fenton's office was in Beverly Hills on Wilshire Boulevard, and Hilary found West Hollywood, which was close by, intriguing. It reminded her of Greenwich Village, with people on Melrose Avenue in jeans and T-shirts as well as suits, ducking into cute coffee places or secondhand clothing shops. Fenton's office manager set Hilary up with a Realtor named Jane Hogan. Jane had raised a family and was a grandmother. Her real estate license was her fifty-fifth birthday present to herself. Now she was turning sixty, and Hilary felt she was in extremely competent hands. Jane had a convertible. She'd pick Hilary up, and off they'd go, the sweet California air blowing in their faces. Hilary and Fenton decided that an apartment complex with a swimming pool would be a good first home. Later on, when hopefully the babies came, they could buy a house with a yard. Jane took Hilary to a number of buildings in Hollywood and West Hollywood, and it didn't take long for Hilary to line up three apartments for Fenton to see. While looking, she and Jane would stop for lunch or tea. Jane had grown up in San Diego but had lived in Los Angeles since attending UCLA, and she generously shared her knowledge of the area. Hilary enjoyed talking to Jane and planned to continue seeing her new friend after the apartment search ended.

They chose a one-bedroom unit in a complex on Fountain Avenue. The apartment was on the third floor, and each floor had a washer and dryer, which Hilary loved. They spent a Saturday picking out some basic furniture.

Hilary was on the job search, sending out résumés to schools in all the surrounding areas. She also advertised herself as a tutor and got some students to work with in their homes after school. She had to learn how to drive quickly to get to these jobs, and she and Fenton purchased a used Toyota Corolla for her. It was a winter white, which reminded her of the cream she loved for her coffee. It was smaller than Fenton's company sedan, and she enjoyed navigating herself around in it.

Fenton was working hard, and his hours were irregular, but whenever he could make it home for dinner, Hilary either cooked or picked up something warm and tasty for them to eat. She would set their new cherrywood dining table with place mats and candles she'd brought from New York and pour glasses of red or white wine.

Hilary got a part-time job substitute teaching at a school in Culver City, and she had a decent amount of kids to tutor. It was good she had the work because Fenton's job seemed to be eating him whole. He left very early most mornings, while Hilary was asleep. She asked him to wake her so they could at least have coffee together, but he said all he could do that early was to shower and leave.

"They have coffee, Danish, rolls—all that stuff at the office because they know we grunts will be in there predawn to do their bidding!"

"But, baby, I miss you when you're out the door before I even open my eyes, and then a lot you don't get home until I'm in bed. I know it's competitive, but what about us? We hardly have any time together lately." Hilary said this kindly, imploringly. She wasn't whiny or bitchy and Fenton took her hand, saying, "I know, babe—I've been a bit preoccupied. I hadn't figured on the workload being so huge and, you're right, competitive. If I'm not willing to put in the time, believe me, others are more than willing to." The job took so much out of Fenton there was not a whole lot left, so their lovemaking was less frequent, which Hilary missed. Still, she wanted to support her husband's career goals. She was glad she and Jane had kept up a friendship and met for lunch when they could. Hilary also met a woman her own age at the library. Alice was ahead of Hilary in line to return some books, and Hilary noticed one of them was one she had read and made a comment. They discussed that book and some others as they exited the library and wound up exchanging phone numbers. Alice worked as the assistant to an established decorator in the area, and so her schedule varied. Hilary enjoyed her company whenever they were able to get together. Alice was also a transplanted New Yorker, having moved to Los Angeles a year before Hilary and Fenton had.

"I was kind of done with the city—I'm not a fan of Mayor Lindsay's—so I came out here to chill. I started helping my boss with the decorating because I heard through a mutual friend she needed someone. It worked out, so I'm here for the time being, and I adore not having winter," Alice told Hilary on their first lunch date. It was a Saturday, and Fenton was at an all-day work retreat an hour away. After lunch, Hilary took herself to the new Century City Mall, thinking she could get in some good walking, which was not easy in Los Angeles. Since she was not really a shopper, she walked the interior from one end to the other. Mainly in her line of sight were mothers wheeling strollers with adorable kids curiously looking around. That started her thinking about her and Fenton starting a family, and her stomach clutched. Just a few nights ago, Fenton had rolled in after 10:00 p.m., exhausted and not even needing food. He said he'd grabbed something near the office around 8:00 p.m. so he could keep working on some client file with unreal deadlines. Half joking, but half not, Hilary said, "How are your children ever going to know you if you don't get home until after they are asleep?" Fenton's half-closed, tired eyes opened wide.

"What are you saying, Hil—you're not pregnant, are you?" His voice was somewhat accusatory, which caught Hilary off guard.

"Well, no, I'm not," she said, wondering why he looked almost freaked by that prospect. They had talked about wanting a family, and not in some distant future. Fenton's shoulders relaxed as he gave her half a smile, his relief palpable.

What was that reaction from him about? Hilary asked herself as she walked the mall. Were his career goals going to take longer to achieve, and so he couldn't even think about starting their family quite yet? But if that were the case, why hadn't he just said so with some encouragement or kindness? He'd been almost hostile and had not mentioned it since. Was he having second thoughts about their marriage, had his feelings for her changed? Involuntary tears welled up in her eyes, and she walked a bit faster, deciding to get out of the baby-filled mall.

She made it into her car and started to cry. What if Fenton was falling out of love with her? She realized that she did feel like she was subtly losing him, but mostly she had thought it was to his demanding job. What if his feelings for her were changing or diminishing separate from work? Maybe being at work had started to appeal to him as a way to not have to be with her. Even on the weekend, he seemed somewhat aloof, although he claimed he was still thinking about the office. They would have a Saturday and Sunday stretched out before them with hours that, for Hilary, could be filled staying in bed upon waking to make unhurried love and then talking about their future plans over breakfast. But as she sat in her car, trying to stop crying, she realized she couldn't remember spending a weekend like that of late. Fenton would need to sleep, period, on a Friday night. Next morning, he'd bolt out of bed to go for a long run outside to "unwind" from the workweek. He'd return and shower, and finally they'd spend some time together. They talked about their jobs, her students, and his associates and sometimes went to a movie or casual dinner. They would get home, fall asleep, or make swift and not very intimate love. Today he was at a retreat, so half their weekend was spent apart. Hilary had stopped crying as she went over this in her mind. She stared out the windshield at the wall of the garage. He hasn't said "I love you" for some time, she thought, not that she expected him to every other day. Did she need to talk to him, ask him directly about his feelings for her? This thought made her cringe and almost start to cry again. That would be so humiliating and feeble. And if nothing had changed on his part, putting him on the spot with a line of demanding questions would probably turn him off.

As she started the car, she decided that the thing to do was absolutely nothing. She could go with the flow of their lives right now. She didn't need to sink herself with doubt and fear.

She shopped for food to make a lovely home-cooked meal for them. Fenton thought the retreat would finish at six and he would be home by seven or so.

Around 7:30, he called to say he was back but having drinks with a few of his work associates.

"We had such an intense day, so we decided to lighten it up with a beer before heading home," he said flatly, offering no apology.

"Well, don't eat, just have that beer, because I've got dinner here all ready to go," she said, trying to sound sweeter than she felt, hoping to mask her disappointment.

"Cool," he said, and hung up.

He took his time and arrived home well after nine. Hilary had gotten so hungry that she'd eaten her salad and some of her baked potato, trying to at least wait on Fenton for steak.

He had clearly had more than one beer. He gave her a kiss on the cheek and went into the bathroom, and after a few minutes, she heard the shower going. She had just about had it by then. It seemed very inconsiderate of him to be so bland about their Saturday night, especially when he'd been gone all day at the retreat.

She did understand about a quick beer even if she wasn't thrilled, but the night had gotten away from her, from them, and he didn't seem to care.

When he came out of the bathroom, he was in a robe.

"Smells good in here. Is dinner still an option? I'm starved!"

"Dinner was never not an option," she said curtly, and then, trying to soften her tone, she added, "I only had salad while waiting, so we can dine together as planned."

With that, she put everything on the table, which had been set for hours, and started to pour wine into his glass.

"No wine for me," he said, waving his hands. "The steaks look great, though. Sorry I was late getting home—glad you waited." She felt warmed hearing this and a bit guilty for having been angry.

"That's OK, honey, I understand. So tell me about the retreat."

By the start of their second year in Los Angeles, Fenton felt he was close to becoming a partner. He had worked on a few high-profile cases with one partner who was definitely advocating for his promotion. Hilary was hopeful that once that happened, they could start to look for a home to buy. She liked their apartment but had continued to feel like their personal, future life was still on a hold until Fenton got his career fully launched. She had actually looked at some homes with Jane, telling her not to let Fenton know. Jane was fine with that and understood that it was a bit premature but that Hilary wanted to get some idea of the housing market.

She took Hilary to the Hollywood Hills. The first house was a Spanish style with three bedrooms and a swimming pool, even though Hilary was not at all sure she wanted a pool. For one thing, it would have to be made child safe with some kind of strong fencing, and Hilary knew she would still worry.

"We're just looking around, hon," Jane said. "No worries, and believe me, clients usually end up with homes we'd never imagined for them at the start! I mainly wanted you to see this type of architecture because it's very popular out here, but your motherly needs will certainly come first. You're not expecting, are you?"

"No," Hilary said quietly.

"I'm sorry—that was a bit nosy of me," Jane said, putting her arm around Hilary as they walked. Hilary wasn't going to say anything more because she feared she'd really open up to Jane if she did. She had gotten used to Fenton not being as gung ho into her as he had been. She made herself busy with her own work and the few friends she'd made. She read a lot of books she took out of the library near their apartment. Whenever she got close to having some kind of talk with Fenton, she got too scared of changing the dynamic of their life, even of losing him, if she put any pressure on him about the future. She knew this was weird since they had started out talking about their future all the time. He was kind to her and loving but not passionately the way he had been. He apologized lots for working late and being dead tired afterward, but he never tried to remedy this, and he didn't seem to miss spending more time with her the way she missed the time with him.

When she got home that day from house hunting, Hilary realized that while she didn't want to open up to Jane, she did feel alone and in need of someone close to talk to, and so she called Ida. Hilary knew Ida usually got home around four in the afternoon and tried her. She answered on the second ring and was glad to hear Hilary's voice.

"Hey, Hil, good to hear from you. You have been on my mind the past few days."

"Well, I need to talk if you have some time now, and if not, tell me when you would."

"I'm good. What's wrong? You sound kind of down."

"I am," Hilary said, and started to cry. "I'm sorry, Ida. I didn't know I'd start crying, but I'm just not happy out here. Fenton has gotten distant in a way I cannot put my finger on, but I don't feel close to him. He works nonstop, gets home late and exhausted, but it's not even that; it's that I don't feel in it with him anymore."

Ida took a breath before she said, "Hilary, I'm so sorry. Have you talked to him about all of this? What has he said?"

"No, I've been afraid to press him, afraid to hear him say he doesn't love me or something like that."

"Hil, you absolutely must talk to him. Tell him what you are feeling and fearing. You have to get some kind of reality check. He may not even be aware of all this. He may think everything is fine, and he's just working his fanny off, you know? Men can get myopic climbing that career ladder. You got to check things out with him, Hilary, no matter how scary that sounds."

"I know you are right, Ida. I so appreciate talking to you and getting your encouragement."

"You have it, honey, so sit this man down and have a much-needed heart-to-heart."

They hung up, and Hilary said she would keep Ida in the loop. She felt relieved to have told her best friend, and she felt ready to have a go at talking to Fenton.

Ironically, he got home at a reasonable hour that very night. She had made a casserole the day before, and they were having leftovers for dinner. They sat at their dining table drinking wine and eating. She had butterflies in her stomach and picked at her food.

"Fenton," she started, shaking, "I need to talk to you about some stuff."

"What stuff?" he said curiously, still eating.

"Well, I feel we have drifted apart some from when we first moved here. I mean, I know you're working really hard, but you used to seem more, I don't know, enthusiastic about us and talking about our future, and for a while now, you don't seem to have that going on as much."

"Do you?" he asked.

"Do I what?"

"Do you have that going on as much as you did?" She looked at him with crinkled eyebrows.

"Yes, I do, of course. Do I seem not to?"

"You've kind of been in your own world lately. I mean, I know I work long hours, but when I'm home you seem to tiptoe around, stay to yourself. Maybe you're not aware of this?"

"I just didn't want to press you, you know, or be a nag, but it's gotten to be too lonely for me not to try to talk about it. I'm really sorry if you felt ignored. I haven't lost any of my love or desire for you, Fenton, not any."

"OK, so then we're good," he said, and went back to his plate. Hilary didn't know what to say next, even though she did not feel resolved. Somehow, he'd turned it around to point at her. She felt no closer to Fenton right now—that much she knew.

"Well, Fenton, I don't know if we're good," she said, staring at him. "I mean, I just told you how I feel, that my feelings for you, for our marriage, are the same as when we started, but I don't know if it's that way for you now, today."

"Look, Hilary, you knew coming out here would be an adjustment. You knew my work would get crazy busy too. I don't think anything is different than what we anticipated. We're making our way out here, aren't we?"

"Yes, we are, of course, but we used to crave being with each other, and I don't feel that coming from you. Fenton, are you still in love with me?" She gulped as she asked this and finally looked away from him. A quiet filled the room. Fenton stopped eating and became still. Finally, he said, "Look, Hilary, I do love you. It's not that. It's just that…" He hesitated. She waited. "It's just that…I do have something going on." Her stomach flipped. Did she want to know what he had going on? This is what she had feared, why she had not wanted to push it. She poured them both some more wine and looked at him. His eyes were staring at the floor. He seemed small.

"I, um…When we got out here," he started, "it was beautiful and sunny and just very free in a way that the East isn't. I found myself feeling loose and unhinged, more so than I had ever imagined, like a chalkboard wiped clean. I truly saw a chalkboard like at school being erased and all this shiny black to dive into." She'd never heard him talk in metaphors like a poet. He was a litigation attorney. She wondered if he had smoked pot.

"Fenton, you sound kind of high to me."

"I'm not. I mean, the wine is nice, but I'm not drunk at all."

"OK," she said, starting to hold her breath for whatever was coming.

"So, feeling this new way out here, I started to check out the strip area, on Sunset. I can't exactly explain how it started, but I ended up parking and walking around the strip, area and, um, I made contact." He stopped and looked at her as he said this word. He seemed to be getting uncomfortable.

"Contact?" she said.

He breathed heavily and said, "I made contact," and then added, "with guys."

"Which guys?" she asked, still not fully getting what he was saying.

"There are places, bars, on the strip where you can pick up guys—if you're a guy, that is. It's sort of a secret that's not once you know about it. You can spend time there or go for a ride up into the hills and have contact." Every time he said "contact," he seemed embarrassed.

"What kind of contact, Fenton? What are you telling me?" she said, sounding a bit panicked.

"I'm saying, Hilary, that I've been picking up men, taking them in my car."

"Taking them up in the hills?" she said, repeating what he'd said.

"Yes." He would not be more graphic. She was starting to hear what he was trying to tell her, and it repulsed her. She knew there were men that did this kind of thing. Homos, fairies were what they were called, and usually they talked with lisps and had high feminine voices and were hairdressers. Her husband, her Fenton, was a man, a lawyer. He wasn't a swish.

"I don't understand," Hilary said, hoping for an explanation that would be more acceptable than what she was thinking.

"I don't understand it exactly myself," he said softly. "I seem to have to do this, like even when I think I will stop, I know I won't."

"Do you get names, exchange phone numbers with these men?" Hilary asked.

"No, not so far at least," Fenton said. "Part of the attraction, I guess you'd call it, is not knowing the person, being strangers."

"And then you just drive back down and the—person—gets out of the car?"

"Yup."

"But you feel like you have to be doing this, like you don't have a choice?" Hilary said, losing some patience.

Fenton looked at her then. His face was immobile. "I guess so," he said. "I mean it feels like that, but I know it is me choosing it."

"Have you told anyone else?" she asked.

"God no, I can't imagine anyone else knowing, but I couldn't keep it from you any longer. I saw that tonight. Actually, I try to get my mind off it except when it's happening."

They cleared the table and did the dishes in silence. When they got into bed, they quietly held each other as they fell asleep.

A few days later, Ida called to check in. When Hilary heard her voice, she froze.

"Hey, girl, how is it going? Did you have your heart-to-heart? Hello, Hilary, are you there?" Ida implored.

Hilary took a breath and said, "Yes, we did speak."

"And?"

"I can't," Hilary said, starting to cry.

"Oh my goodness, Hilary, what?" Ida said. "Get some tissue and try to calm yourself enough to talk to me." Hilary followed Ida's instructions, not sure of what she would say. For one thing, she felt she had to protect Fenton from the stigma of what he had told her, even though she needed to talk to someone she trusted.

"Ida, I don't think I can talk about this now, but I appreciate knowing you are there for me."

"Of course I am, Hilary. I'm sorry you are dealing with whatever it is on your own. You know I can keep a confidence to the grave, right?" Hilary did know this, as could she.

"Well," she said, deciding that maybe this would help both her and Fenton in some way. "Well, Ida, what's going on is that Fenton…" She just couldn't say the thing he was doing.

"Fenton, what, wants to break up?" Ida asked, trying to fill in the blank.

"No, not now, anyhow," Hilary said, taking a breath. "He likes to…I mean, he has this thing he does out here…with men."

"He does something with men?" Ida asked.

"Yes," Hilary said, starting to cry again.

A few seconds passed, and then Ida said, "You mean sexual stuff?"

"Yes, I mean he didn't spell it out, but that's it, what's going on."

"Does he have a boyfriend?"

"No, it's not like that; it's more just random?" Hilary felt so embarrassed.

"OK, OK, well, that's some kind of a shocker, I'd say." Ida was speechless for a moment and then added, "But at least he told you; you two are talking. That's supposed to be the most important thing in a relationship, being honest and open, right?" She tried to sound hopeful while still taken aback.

"I don't know. I mean, I guess it's better that I know, but I'm so upset. Plus I am pretty disgusted by him doing this stuff. That's not the man I thought I married."

"Yeah, I have to say Fenton never struck me as one of those kind of, well, you know. But then it seems they had to hide in the past but are starting to be more public since a few years ago—that thing at Stonewall Inn in the city?"

"Ida, I don't think he's one of those kind. That riot at Stonewall was men living with men, having boyfriends, doing their lives like that. I mean, I think Fenton is just checking out some kind of scene here at the strip on Sunset. At least that's how he described it to me," Hilary said, feeling defensive.

"OK, so maybe it's just a phase, but, you know, Hil, it may be more," Ida said carefully.

"I know," Hilary said, tearing up.

"Do you two…? I mean, I am not trying to pry, but…"

"I know what you're asking. We do make love sometimes, not a lot and not as passionately at all. That's why I asked him what was going on. I mean, maybe he's both ways—there's a term for that I think. But I don't know if I can live like that, sharing him with strange men."

"Hilary, do not get ahead of yourself, please. Like I said, it's good you two have cards on the table for now, and you can work things out if they are meant to be—you have to believe that."

"And if they're not, then what do I do with my life?"

"We don't have to go there right now, Hil—honestly, we don't," Ida said firmly.

Fenton wiped his lips with some tissue as the man next to him in his car zipped up his fly.

"That was fun," the man said. "You've got a wicked mouth there. My turn!"

Fenton felt an erection coming and opened his pants. He leaned back and closed his eyes. After, he started his car and pulled back onto the road.

"Where can I drop you?" he asked the man.

"Just back on Sunset at La Cienega, if that's cool." They rode in silence to the drop-off point. The man got out and gave a slight wave before he walked away. Fenton knew he'd probably see him again if he kept cruising the strip.

In fact, he'd probably see the others if he came back for seconds and thirds.

That could be damaging to his position at the firm. So far, he had not given his name or any other information to these men. It seemed like the way it worked, and Fenton was glad. Even in the bars, if he went to the men's room with a man, the deed was done anonymously. As much as these relations turned him on, Fenton was beginning to fear all the exposure. At first, he was connecting this way once in ten days, if that. Then, after he told Hilary about it, for some reason he had needed to make connections at least once a week or more. He knew a few of the bartenders recognized him when he came in as a patron, even without knowing his name. He, too, was starting to see "familiar" faces at these places. He had decided not to go back to a few, where he felt he had overstayed his welcome.

Telling Hilary had also driven him inward. He had been putting the encounters out of his mind. Now, he thought about them and tried to understand.

He remembered he had noticed certain boys in high school and college who were attractive. He had felt jealous of their good looks. Had those good looks turned him on sexually? He could not clearly recall, but if so, he definitely would not have admitted it to himself. Then, the idea was to have sex with girls, preferably pretty ones with curves. At law school he was mainly focused on his studies while also working to put himself through. He had, however, had one professor whom he now realized he might have wanted physically. At the time, he thought of it as his need for a father figure since he and his parents were estranged. He hadn't dated that many women but had enjoyed the sex he had with them, for the most part. With Hilary, it was so much more than having sex. It was expressing the love he felt for her. He had wanted to marry her without hesitation.

His first time, he had gone into a bar that seemed to cater to men and not women. The men were talking and laughing and drinking and being physical with one another but in no way like being in a locker room. Fenton felt thrilled from the moment he was inside. He ordered a beer while standing at the bar because all the stools were occupied. As he reached for his drink, the man seated to the left of him said, "Enjoy your brew, handsome!" Fenton looked at the man, who was younger than he, maybe early twenties, with thick brown hair falling over his eyes, which twinkled at Fenton mischievously. Fenton mumbled thanks as he backed away from the bar, but the man swiveled his stool so as to stare at him.

This guy is flirting with me, Fenton realized. The thought excited him. So now what do I do? he thought as the man on the stool turned back around to face the bar. As he did so, the seat next to him became available, and Fenton found himself taking it. He sipped his beer and looked straight ahead, his heart beating faster. The man turned to him, saying, "I don't think I've seen you here before."

"You haven't," Fenton said quietly.

"Well then, it's my lucky night. Can I show you around?"

Fenton had only finished half his beer, but when the man took his hand and led him off the stool, toward the back where the restrooms were, he followed, feeling like he was sleepwalking.

The restroom was a single, and the man locked it and turned to Fenton.

"First time, sailor?" he asked gently. Fenton nodded. "Just relax, and I'll do the heavy lifting," the man said, and then took Fenton in his arms and kissed him, his tongue parting Fenton's lips. Fenton opened his mouth, suddenly hungry for the tongue, hungry like he had never felt before.

When the man got on his knees and started giving him a blow job, Fenton had come fast and felt embarrassed, saying, "I'm sorry, I just lost control—didn't mean to make a mess."

"Yeah, well, it can be like that when you're not accustomed to this, and I guess I knew this might happen, but you're so handsome, I just had to taste you."

"I have not ever, but if you want I can, you know, return the favor?" Fenton said, searching for words that he'd never spoken.

"No, that's OK, sailor. I figure I did my good deed for today; you're a virgin no more, and maybe we'll do this again some time." With that, he exited the bathroom.

Fenton relocked the door, pissed, and cleaned himself. He stood there a bit shaken until someone was trying the door. When he opened it, there were two men waiting to go in. He walked directly toward the main entrance, not looking around, and left. When he got in his car, he sat for a while before starting it. Hilary was at home with dinner waiting. He loved his wife, but kissing the strange man had made him feel so alive. In that bathroom he had felt aroused the way he had when he'd started having wet dreams. And just like those dreams happened to him beyond his control, this whole new chapter in his life seemed to be writing itself until he told Hilary. At that moment he had gained control. Telling her was saying, "This is who I am, and this is what I do." He could see his wife was devastated, even though she tried to keep herself together. A few nights later, she asked him if he still wanted to be married to her. He said yes, adding, "I love you, Hilary. You're my family. I don't even know the names of these guys—it's not personal at all."

"So what makes you keep doing it?" she asked.

"It's some kind of very strong desire to physically connect right then and there, a powerful momentary turn-on, and then it's over, almost like it never happened." He said this looking at her, forcing himself to. He wanted her to understand, to still love him.

She started to cry and said, "Fenton, can't you just stop?"

He was silent for minutes before he said, "I don't want to stop, but I so wish I did."

Hilary was on a kind of a pause after that. She kept to her routine, working part time at the school, tutoring students, shopping for food, preparing dinner for herself and Fenton. When he came in time to eat with her, they sat across from each other and talked of simple things like work, the weather, the meal they were sharing. Eventually, one or the other would retire to the bedroom for a shower and then sleep. The other would follow in time but not right away. They were being gentle with each other, careful not to take a step in any direction just yet. Their marriage had undergone something undefined but with side effects nevertheless. Hilary found herself in tears at odd, unexpected moments. She would be driving back from school or an errand, and suddenly tears were streaming down her face, blurring her vision so that she would have to blink a lot or pull the car over to the side of the road, burying her face in her arms crossed over the steering wheel, weeping loudly, her body shaking, until she could soothe herself with deep breaths that replaced the gasps.

A week after he said he wasn't stopping, Fenton got home in time for dinner. Hilary had broiled salmon and steamed spinach for a simple, healthy meal. As they began to eat, he looked at her, saying, "Hilary, listen we have a situation that's come up." Hilary stiffened at the ominous tone in his voice.

"What is it?" she asked.

"Bob and Marlene are in town. He's being transferred here next month, and they are looking for a home to rent. They want to get together for dinner and hear all about our life out here. Have you been in touch with Marlene?"

"Only a few phone calls since we got here. I have not spoken to her since…" She left the rest unsaid.

"OK, well, the thing is, I need to make this happen. Bob is important to me. He is already a partner and thinks I should be too." He looked so vulnerable, scared almost of what she would say. She was moved by this but had no desire to have power over him or his job. She wanted them to be OK, period, and they were not.

"If you want me to go on some charade dinner with them where we act like everything's hunky-dory, I guess I can try to pull that off. I like Bob and Marlene, but right now we are not exactly couple material."

"Yeah, I know," he said.

"And to be honest, Fenton, since you're still so on track with your career goals, what are your goals for us? I care way more about that right now than you making partner, no offense," she said somewhat angrily.

"Look, Hil, I will get together with them myself. I'll tell them you're under the weather at the moment or something. You won't have to deal, all right?"

"No, it's not all right—did you not hear what I just said about your job versus us?"

"Look, my job is what keeps us going financially. Besides which, I didn't spend all this time first at law school, now at the firm to just chuck it or take my eye off the ball, and that has nothing to do with this personal thing going on with me, with us."

"Well, what are your goals where we are concerned, if you even have any?" she asked.

"I want it to be like it was, Hil, I really do, but I also know it is not, and I don't know how to get back to being that guy."

"You don't want to get back to being that guy!" she said bitterly. They were at their impasse again. After a few moments, she said calmly, "Maybe you should talk to a doctor or a shrink about this, you know?"

He shook his head aggressively, saying, "No, I don't think so. If any of this were to get out, get back to the firm…" He shuddered.

"But doctors have to keep things totally confidential, Fenton. Besides, the way you are carrying on, anyone could find out any time—you must realize that."

He rose, shoving his chair back, leaving his plate, and went into the bedroom.

Soon she heard the shower and knew she had pushed a button and there would be no more talking this evening. So be it, she thought. We cannot go on like this; I cannot go on like this. I love this man, and I even feel sorry for what is going on with him, but I am also furious at him and hurt. And at this point, her tears were back.

Maybe I should talk to someone professional, she thought. Maybe I should confide to a shrink or doctor or someone about our situation. She decided she would at least call Ida because Ida already knew. She would start with her.

The next day, Hilary called Ida in the late afternoon, hoping she would reach her.

Ida was home.

"Hey, Hilary, good to hear your voice. How are you?" Hilary had so wanted to have a composed conversation, but as she started to speak, her voice cracked, and she was crying yet again.

"Sorry, Ida, I am sort of losing it, I have to admit. Fenton is still picking up men and says he doesn't want to stop and he wishes he wanted to, but he doesn't. I mean, honestly, Ida, if he was fooling around with another woman, I would be bummed for sure, but I would feel like I had a chance to win him back, compete, you know?"

"Hilary, do you think Fenton was latent and that this is the real him? Because from what I know, which is not a whole lot, if that is the case, the genie may be out of the bottle, and this might be it. Can he talk to a professional about this, get some counseling?"

"Ida, that is exactly what I suggested, but he is so paranoid about anyone finding out—oh, and he doesn't know I'm talking to you, so he thinks no one knows. His main concern isn't even our marriage; his main concern is his job, making partner, not having anyone at his firm find out!" It was such a relief to be sharing what her life had become with someone she could trust.

"I get that. I know how much his career means to him; plus, that's an area of his life he can still control, whereas this seems out of his control. It's too bad he won't talk to someone. What about the two of you having some marriage counseling. Would he do that, do you think?"

"I don't know; it would still be telling someone about what he's been doing. I will ask him, though. I am sure we are not the first couple to be dealing with something like this."

Fenton got home late, and they did not talk. Hilary was having lunch with Jane the next day and was not looking forward to it. She knew she had to put on a game face. Jane was trying to show Hilary some homes for sale that had come on the market, thinking that Hilary and Fenton were getting ready to take the next step home wise. At lunch, Jane had a folder of new listings, and Hilary took it and said she would look through them.

"We need to see someone and talk about what's going on, maybe a marriage counselor," Hilary said as she and Fenton shared a quiet dinner at home a few nights later. His head jerked slightly as she spoke, and he kept eating, looking at his food as if he wanted her words to evaporate into the air.

"Fenton, I just said something. What do you think?" He looked up and gave her a cold stare. "What?" she said. "Please talk to me."

"I have already told you, I am not going to any person and talking about my very personal situation that I am trying to work through," he said. "Now you can wait with me, see where we get, or not Hilary. I'm not going to tell you what you should do. The truth is, I don't know what's going to happen to us. I know I love you, but I am not the man I was the day we married. I think I just need to stay my own course right now, and I am hoping, praying actually, that this stuff I'm doing doesn't wreck my career and all I can—"

"Your fucking career," Hilary exploded. "Is that all you care about? You just said you love me. Does that mean you at all care about us? I saw Jane this week, and she gave me a fistful of house listings since she figures we're ready to start a family." Tears had started down her cheeks. Fenton took a gulp of wine.

"I'm saying that I love you, but I don't know about us, our life together. I'm saying I don't think I can go backward even though going forward is scary as hell. I know this is hurting you big time, Hil, and believe it or not, I am so sorry that I'm the cause of your pain. I didn't plan for this to happen, although I think this may have been with me from when I was a kid. I got good at swallowing it, like when you take bad medicine while you hold your breath, but now I'm throwing it up."

"So, be honest, is staying together right now more about you posing like you're a married man for your career or because you really hope to work it out with me?" Hilary asked, trembling.

"I am trying to figure it all out, but you are not wrong about how acting like a married man, being seen as one, helps me at work."

"Do you know anyone at your firm who is homosexual?" The word just came out of her mouth, and though he winced ever so slightly, he seemed to know it was a fair question.

"There is one paralegal who seems a bit that way, but I can't say for sure. I don't work directly with him, and none of the other guys have said anything."

At least they were having honest exchanges. If her life was going to fall apart, she wanted to understand how it decomposed. They spent the rest of the night talking softly about simple things, going to bed not touching but feeling close.

Hilary managed to get through dinner with Bob and Marlene. Even Fenton seemed to be barely getting by with them as he fielded their questions about neighborhoods in which to live, things to do in year-round warm weather, and how the office worked in Los Angeles versus Manhattan.

When they got home, Fenton said, "Thanks for tonight, Hil. I know it was hard, but you were great, and I do appreciate it. "

"Yeah, well, you're welcome, Fenton, but don't be surprised if Bob asks you if everything is OK with us. We both seemed kind of strained."

If Bob had mentioned anything, Fenton had not told Hilary in the weeks that followed. Once Bob joined the Los Angeles office, Fenton felt hopeful he would make partner before the end of the year.

It was the holiday season, and Hilary hated it. She had been enthusiastic in years past and had gotten a small artificial tree their first Christmas in Los Angeles.

She still had not set it up, and it was mid-December. She doubted she would bother. In their most recent conversation, Hilary told Ida that she planned to coast for a while, get through the holidays, and then see.

Hilary was off from school until the new year, so she had even more time on her hands. She made a lunch date with Alice, whom she had not seen for a while.

They met at Hamburger Hamlet on Sunset Boulevard. Alice was working on a home in Bel Air, some famous client whose name she could not divulge.

"Business has been so good. I'm moving to a bigger place in the new year. What about you, weren't you guys going to get out of your apartment, move into a house?" she asked while dipping a French fry into ketchup.

Hilary waited a beat to answer and then said, "Yes, I think we will get to that eventually, but right now my husband is working so much; he needs to relax when he's off, and house hunting feels like a job."

When they parted, Hilary felt forlorn. Alice was nice, but Hilary felt lonely spending time with her, having to put on a facade about her life. It was the same with Jane. At this point, Hilary thought, I am going to keep to myself, talk to Ida when I need to, and read a bunch of engaging books until school starts up.

The firm had a holiday cocktail party. When she arrived, the restaurant was packed, but she found Fenton with a glass of wine in his hand standing with Bob Carter and some other men. Marlene had opted out of coming because a close friend of hers from New York was in town and leaving the next day. Bob gave Hilary a warm hug, which made her feel relieved for Fenton.

She did want him to make partner, she thought. She had a better time than she had anticipated. She met many of Fenton's associates who all seemed fond of Fenton and pleased to make her acquaintance. The very next day, he was told he had made partner. He called Hilary to give her his exciting news, adding that everyone enjoyed seeing her at the party. Finally, there was some joy in their lives, she thought as she hung up the phone. She would make a celebratory dinner for Fenton and start with a champagne toast. Maybe things would get better in 1972.

As a partner, Fenton had even more of a workload. The firm had increased its clientele in 1971, becoming a landing place for actors, actresses, musicians, and anyone needing professional advice in the area of entertainment law. Working more with artistic clients, even at times hippies, had given Fenton a degree of comfort at his job. These clients were not straitlaced or conservative. They were "groovy" and seemed more permissive in their attitudes about things like alcohol, pot, sex, clothes, hairstyles, and social behavior. Expressions like "Whatever turns you on, man" were said about all kinds of situations. A rock band Fenton represented joked in his office about the groupies that followed them on the road and the orgy-like parties that followed their performances on stage. Fenton didn't say much when hearing this; he would just nod and smile and get back on the track of whatever business he was doing with them, but inside, he felt this climate in step with his own personal situation. He had let go out here, exploring himself in ways that were starting to feel more acceptable. He could be in a store to buy jeans and sense someone looking at him in just such a way that had become code. Within minutes, he and the "someone" would be outside, going to a park or getting in the car and parking somewhere more private for a hot, engaging, and purely physical exchange. The highlight of his day came with these fleeting but powerful connections. His life at home was flat, even sad. Hilary had started the new year with some kind of hope that as the ball dropped, their lives would change back to what they had been, even though Fenton had not given her any indication that he was getting over his circumstance. That's how he phrased it in his mind, his "circumstance." It seemed less offensive, but he knew he was kidding himself. He had started to understand that he wasn't changing back. Unlike the frog prince in that fairy tale he'd liked as a kid, he was staying the frog, and no amount of kissing his wife could work him back into the handsome man who had been her prince. He had lost something they had come to California with—a family of two that would become more. Sometimes, he missed what he had had with Hilary as much as he imagined she did. Still, he knew he was not that person, even if she was. He wasn't as afraid of being found out, although he still worked diligently to project his married-man image. The paralegal he had mentioned to Hilary had become outward about his sexual preference for men, and even though it was a point of some sneering gossip at the office, the paralegal still had his job. Dylan had it right, Fenton thought, "The times, they are a-changin'!"

The new year had been a bust so far, and Hilary was feeling low. Fenton was doing his "thing" and seeming less conflicted about it, from what she could tell. They hadn't talked about their situation in a while, but she knew it was not a "till death do us part" one anymore. Her hope starting the new year had lost steam by February. She was going through the motions of a person living a life, but she felt ancient as she did. She could not believe she was only in her twenties. She and Fenton were living like roommates, and the saddest part to her was that it was starting to feel normal.

"At this point, Hil, I think you and Fenton are living a lie," Ida had said bluntly a few days before. "I mean, if that's what you both want, so be it, but you have been suffering."

"I know, Ida. I feel in a limbo with Fenton, with our life together so different. Having said this, I'm not sure I want to give it up, even though I desperately want our former life back. Does that make sense?"

"Of course. You're not ready to have nothing instead of the something you still have. I get that; I just want you to remember that you are a young, beautiful woman with your whole life ahead of you." Hilary always felt better after talking with Ida, and as she hung up, she tried to imagine herself single. Would she stay in LA or head back East, which still felt like home? She thought about the Hilary she was before she'd met Fenton. She liked her life well enough then, hadn't been looking to marry yet. She had enjoyed teaching, her friends, taking long walks in Central Park, getting coffee and cookies at the local bakery. Could she be that person again? She didn't believe so. She had loved meeting Fenton, falling in love with him and becoming his wife. She had embraced it all without reservation. The idea of being an "I" again instead of a "we" depressed her, even though in truth she and Fenton were no longer a "we." She would not be single anyhow; she would be a divorcée, and that had a taste of failure and damaged goods. She knew this sounded like people much older than she was, but those views had found their way to her from the 1950s, even though women got divorced a lot more frequently now. Still, no one looks forward to being a divorcée, do they? she wondered.

It was almost Valentine's Day, and Hilary had gotten Fenton a friendly but not romantic card. The actual day was a workday, Monday. Fenton suggested dinner out, and she wondered if that was so he could mention it at the office. Still, it sounded better than being home, so she made a reservation at Musso & Frank Grill, an old-time restaurant on Hollywood Boulevard that reminded her of New York. The place was decorated with crepe paper hearts and roses at each table.

They ordered a bottle of wine, and when the first glasses were poured, Fenton raised his so she lifted her glass too. He smiled and clinked his glass to hers with a nod, then took a sip of wine. Hilary didn't expect the kind of loving toast he had been so great at making, but his inability to say anything leveled her. They had an awkward, expensive dinner and ignored the hearts and flowers around them. Fenton paid, and Hilary thanked him as if they were on a first date. They didn't speak in the car, but once inside their apartment, Fenton took her hand and led her to the couch.

"Hilary, I know dinner was tough for both of us. You have been my one and only valentine, so I wanted to go out tonight, but I know we both could feel how things have changed."

"You have changed, Fenton, not things," she pointed out, tired.

"OK, yes, the change came from me, but now things are changed for us."

"And you're OK with that, am I right?" she said.

"Yes, you are." They sat quietly, letting the air hold the truth.

Hilary got up and went into the bedroom. The card she had gotten was in a drawer for good.

By March, they were passing each other in and out of the apartment. Hilary bought prepared food dinners and had them early and alone. Fenton worked late and ate before getting home exhausted and ready to crash. Ida had been right about how couples could live apart while staying together in the image of a marriage. Friends and coworkers around the couple have no idea that anything so separate is going on. Ida said in these cases, everyone that knows the couple is absolutely shocked when they announce they are breaking up. Everyone except the man and woman who have been broken up for so long already, Hilary thought. Ida suggested Hilary take a trip to visit her in Florida during the school spring break, and Hilary accepted. She told Fenton, and he said that sounded like fun. There was no mention of having to check in with each other, so once Hilary got there, she put her life in Los Angeles out of her mind. She relaxed, enjoyed the humid warmth, and swam in the pool at Ida's complex.

"Do you swim at your pool in LA?" Ida asked.

"You know, I hardly ever do. I'm busy during the day, and it gets cool in the late afternoon. I am not a fan of dry air that makes my skin feel like paper. People out there rave about no humidity, but I like moisture in the air. Go figure," Hilary said, laughing and feeling lighter than she had in a long time.

They ate stone crabs and took walks on the beach. Ida arranged a casual dinner in Hilary's honor so she could meet Ida's Florida friends. They were an adorable group of mainly ladies and a few men of different ages and situations whom Ida had gotten to know over the past five years. The week flew by, and on her last evening, Hilary was sorry to be packing her things.

Fenton met someone in March. He had taken the man's phone number. Fenton had not disclosed where he worked and had not given the man, Gabriel, any other information about himself other than his first name. He had called Gabriel a few days after they met in a Ralph's supermarket and then gone for a drive. Gabriel was a bartender, so he was around during the day. He lived alone in an apartment not far from Fenton's office. They got together at the apartment for lunchtime rendezvous. Fenton was keyed up about Gabriel. He was starting to get to know someone who was like him; they were sharing their secret needs with each other. He had not given Gabriel his last name or told him what he did for a living or that he was married. Gabriel didn't seem curious about this. When they got together, Fenton's time was tight because of work, so they would talk a little and then get physical. While Hilary was in Florida, Fenton had seen Gabriel for an evening when he didn't have to tend bar. They ordered in food and talked more than they ever had before having sex. Fenton left for home feeling invigorated but also nervous. He was stepping over lines in every direction. He was conscious of always keeping his pants close by when at Gabriel's and making sure to only use the bathroom when he was wearing his pants because his wallet was in the back pocket with his ID, driver's license, and business cards. He was being so intimate with this man and yet not wanting Gabriel to know anything about his identity. He did not believe he could continue seeing Gabriel. What Fenton did know was that his marriage to Hilary was in his past, and he needed to deal with that. He could be a divorced man in his office; that wouldn't get heads turned around.

The day before Hilary returned from Florida, Fenton saw Gabriel at lunchtime and told him that he would not be contacting him again. Gabriel took a deep breath and said, "Yeah, man, I figured this was coming. You aren't, you know, comfortable. I saw that right off. Hey, I'm not either, so I thought maybe we could keep it private between us, but that's easier said than done."

That night, as Fenton stood in the living room of the apartment he and Hilary shared, he felt unmoored.

On the plane home, Hilary ordered a gin and tonic. Ida had suggested this, pointing out it was a long flight and a cocktail would be relaxing. Hilary had a window seat, and she lifted the shade as she sipped her drink and saw a white, puffy cloud line that bordered a cornflower-blue sky. She had spoken to Fenton the day before to touch base and give him her flight information. He would be picking her up at LAX. He sounded preoccupied, which could have been work related, but Hilary sensed he had not missed her. She hadn't missed him either because what was there to miss now? She felt tears fill her eyes but blinked them away. She saw that there could be life after Fenton. Like Ida, she was a qualified teacher and could get credentialed in any state. She had an impressive résumé and could certainly be self-supporting again. Ida said she'd met a few divorcées, both men and women, and it wasn't such a stigma now as it would have been for their parents' generation. Hilary was finally feeling a bit hopeful looking out the window.

In the car, coming back from the airport, she told Fenton about her week away, and he filled her in on some of his office gossip. He dropped her off, needing to get back to work. He said there was a barbecued chicken and some prepared salads in the fridge for her and he'd have that, too, whenever he got back, but it would be late.

Hilary unpacked her bag and did laundry from the trip. She was asleep when Fenton got home. The next night, as they sat across from each other eating a pizza they had ordered, he said, "While you were away, I had some time to think. Maybe you did too?" She nodded yes. "Thing is, Hil, I don't think this is a phase with me. I don't know if it's for the rest of my life, but it could be. I don't want to lose you in my life. You are my best friend and my only confidant, but I know that's not fair to you." Again, she nodded.

When he didn't say anything more for a few minutes, she said, "So, Fenton, what should we do now? I love you, but I cannot live like this, in a marriage that is, according to you, not fixable." For the first time since all of this had begun, Fenton had tears starting to stream down his face.

"I'm so sorry, Hilary. I just can't fit myself back into that person. I think even before I met you, I had some sense deep down, but I kept trying to be, um, that, that guy you met and fell in love with. I wanted to be him so much. I wanted…" His voice broke off into sobs. Hilary rose and went to him. She could be the strong one. She had turned a corner, maybe in Florida, maybe before that. No matter.

In May, they separated, and Fenton moved out of the apartment. They agreed on a simple divorce that did not require more legal help than what Fenton could provide. He stressed to Hilary that she had the right to her own attorney, but she said she trusted him to work out the details. They did not own property, and she didn't want alimony from him even if she were entitled to it; she wanted to be entirely independent. The apartment lease was up in August. She was not going to renew it. She gave notice at her job and to the students she tutored. She would move to New York or Florida. She and Fenton decided to say that they were amicable but just not all that compatible and that she in particular wanted to return to the East Coast. Fenton's coworkers were surprised but sympathetic and wished him and Hilary well.

"At least you two didn't start a family—man—you dodged that bullet," Bob Carter said to Fenton. "Having a baby is wonderful if your marriage is good, but it's got to be a real bummer if not." He and Marlene were expecting their first child in the fall.

"Yes, Bob, that is one blessing in this, for sure. I will just have to be the best uncle your kid will ever know," Fenton said, feeling the truth of his words.

In June, when school let out, Hilary made a trip east to New York City. She saw a few friends whom she'd known, but they were married and had moved into the suburbs and started families. Also, Hilary realized she had gotten comfortable not living with winter, and so a climate like Florida's seemed preferable. Finally, there was such a difference in the cost of living, which she could not ignore. New York was so much more expensive. She returned to LA having made the decision to try Florida. Her plan was to pack up her car and drive across the country. She would leave the first week of August and stay with Ida just long enough to find an apartment of her own.

Jane invited Hilary to her home for a Fourth of July barbecue. Jane had been pretty shocked about Hilary and Fenton's divorce but wanted to be supportive. Hilary was glad to have a plan because holidays, she had realized over Memorial Day weekend, would have to be navigated now that she was alone. She was home by ten. She had called Fenton the week before to tell him her plan to move to Florida. Getting into bed, she wondered what he had done for July 4. Probably something with the Carters, she thought. Marlene had called Hilary to say how sorry they both were, and Hilary had thanked her and said it was definitely for the best. Then, she had added congratulations on the pregnancy and wished her and Bob well.

Her drive cross-country was nice but lonely. She had areas where the radio music was good, but many where there was no reception. That's when it was harder for her to keep her mind on the road, but she did, determined to look forward, not backward. Ida gave her a huge hug when she arrived and took her out for a scrumptious meal.

Fenton had called Hilary the night before she left LA to wish her well on her drive. She had not spoken to him since. She figured she'd check in with him at some point to see how he was doing, or vice versa, but for now she was trying to let go of all that had been. She didn't think she was the first wife whose husband turned out to be a homosexual. Ida said she had heard through a friend about a woman dealing with the same issue, but that woman had been married eight years and had two children.

Hilary found a cute apartment near Ida's building, got furniture, and found a decent teaching job in Boca Raton, which wasn't too far a commute. She made some friends at her job and also merged into Ida's social group.

She mailed Fenton a postcard with her new address and phone number. The Tuesday before Thanksgiving, he called her at home in the evening.

"Hilary, it's me, Fenton," he said, as if she might not recognize his voice.

"Hi, Fenton, this is a nice surprise. Are you at work? It's four p.m. where you are."

"No, I'm home now. I had a client appointment out of the office that finished early. I have wanted to call and see how you are, but by the time I get home, you're asleep. So how are you doing?"

"I'm good, thanks. Life here is going reasonably well, I must say. I live near Ida, who has been wonderful. I like my job, and Florida is OK—not the most stimulating place but even keel which for now is fine. How about you?"

"I'm doing OK" he said. "I have good days and not-so-good days."

"Have you told anyone about your—what is going on with you?" she asked hesitantly, not wanting to put him on the spot.

"So far no, but I am not as afraid as I was."

"That's promising," she said. She could hear him taking a breath.

"Hilary, it's good to hear your voice."

"Likewise," she said, feeling warm.

"I care about you, Hil. That part hasn't changed, and I'm so glad you're doing well," he said.

"Thanks, Fenton. I care about you too," she said, knowing she always would.

They promised to keep in touch. Hilary placed the phone in its cradle, her eyes dry and clear.

After

Six weeks after Myrna's mother, Ann, had passed away, her voice popped into Myrna's head, saying, "Devon isn't for you, dear." Myrna had turned toward the door and then remembered her mother wasn't, couldn't actually be there. She sat on her bed thinking, You seemed to like him when you met him, Mom—why have you turned? Myrna and Devon were living together. He'd shown up at her apartment with a backpack and a suitcase a few days earlier. Was that why her mother had chimed in?

She hadn't planned on living with Devon any more than she'd planned to be working in a flower shop. It was a summer job when she needed money. She'd finished two years at Fairleigh Dickinson University and figured she'd keep going and maybe end up a teacher. Then in August, she deferred returning to school. She liked not having homework and deadlines for papers. She decided to keep the job another year and then see. Toward the end of that year, her mother became ill. Her boss let her work part time so she could care for Ann at home until she had to be hospitalized. Myrna was the only child, and her parents were divorced. Until she was ten, though, they'd been a family.

Her father played trumpet in a band that traveled part of the time. Her mother taught at the high school and took care of Myrna. When her father was home, Myrna was not allowed to go near his trumpet. It was the thing he loved the most. Myrna loved Pearl like that. She hadn't named her; the doll makers had.

She still had Pearl. After Devon moved in, she climbed on a stool in what had become their closet and checked her. Then she got a towel, wrapped Pearl in it, and laid her back on the shelf.

When Myrna was ten, Pearl got run over by a car. Myrna was roller-skating a block from her home, holding Pearl in her right arm. She was going fast because she was good. A chip in the sidewalk trapped her left skate, and she fell to the ground, flinging Pearl into the street just as a car turned onto it. The driver didn't stop and probably didn't know he'd hit anything since Pearl was soft like a Raggedy Ann. Myrna's arm had been broken, and she had to have it set in a cast.

"Can you fix Pearl too?" Myrna asked the doctor.

"Well, no, I can't because this is a people's hospital, but there are doll hospitals for your little friend."

Pearl was mailed in a cardboard box and spent more than a month away. Myrna wrote to her. When she received letters in return, she was thrilled. Before Ann died, Myrna thanked her for writing them.

A few months after her skating accident, her father stopped coming home. He called from the road and told her mother he had to "start over." Myrna had answered the phone.

"Pearl's home, Daddy. She's all better now."

"That's great, Myrn. Put your mama on OK, honey?" Myrna was bringing Pearl to talk to her dad when her mother hung up the phone, tears flooding her eyes. Myrna had never seen her mother or any grown-up cry. She thought that was what children did because they were little.

Her parents divorced, and eventually her father settled in Arizona and lived with a woman he later married. He phoned Myrna infrequently and sent presents on her birthday and at Christmas.

When Ann died, Myrna called her father. She was surprised when he said he was coming to the funeral. She told him it wasn't necessary, that she could handle things.

"I'm just coming to pay my respects," he said. "I won't get in the way."

Myrna arranged white lilies for Ann's coffin. At the church, she introduced her dad and his wife, Fran, to Devon.

After the burial, they gathered at Ann's for refreshments.

"How long have you been seeing Devon?" her father asked when he and Myrna were by themselves.

"Going on a year."

"Have you met his family?"

"His father's dead. I met his mother once when she visited from New Orleans. That's where they're from."

"Does he play an instrument? He's from Dixieland."

"I don't think he does."

"How about you, do you play any music?"

"Not so far. Mom left her piano to me, so maybe I'll learn." Her father looked at her hands.

"They could grace a keyboard. Just have to trim the nails some."

"Thanks for your vote of confidence," Myrna said, feeling suddenly mean.

Since the funeral, her father had called sporadically to see how she was doing. The first time Devon answered the phone, it was her father. When Myrna picked up, he asked if Devon lived there too.

"Actually he does," Myrna said lightly.

"Does that mean I'll be giving you away anytime soon?" Myrna shrugged. "Hello, Myrn, you there?"

"How's Fran?"

"Great, she's putting a lot of time into her new business, but I'll be traveling again, so it'll keep her busy. Did you sell the house yet?" A gear switch, but she had expected it. Her father seemed to think he was entitled to some of the money from Ann's home. The last time he'd called, he had mentioned the fact that his savings had gone as the down payment twenty-six years before.

"Of course, in the divorce," he'd said, "I gave your mama the place for you both." Myrna wasn't giving him a dime—not now at least, not unless he was out on the street.

"No, it's a slow market. We've had a few people who seemed interested." One had made an offer, and she'd countered. She hadn't told Devon.

"Well, keep me posted." Myrna hung up and laughed.

"What's so funny?" Devon asked from the living room.

"My dad wants to know when he'll be giving me away."

"I guess that means he approves of me," Devon said as she came in.

"Do you care?"

"Sure, somewhat—you know, the normal amount."

"No, you don't know, dear," her mother's voice prompted in Myrna's mind.

"No, I don't know—what does that mean, the 'normal amount'? You hardly know my dad—I hardly know him for God's sake. What is the nature of your caring what he thinks?" Devon looked at her, his eyebrows crinkled.

"That time of the month, huh, babe."

"Not remotely. And even if it were, that's not an answer."

"Good work, honey," Ann's voice coached.

"Well, actually, I could give a crap what your father thinks about me. But I do care what he thinks about us since he is your dad—for real, even though you two aren't close." He got up and walked around the room, stopping at the window. He stared at the sky, muted by dusk. He's thinking about his own dad, Myrna thought. Now what, Mom? She came next to him.

"I get it," she said softly. He turned and drew her against him.

"So your dad thinks we should get married?" he said, taking her in his arms. He wanted to make love. She could do it or not do it. He took her face in his hands and kissed her.

"Let's lie down," he whispered. He led her to their bed, and she sat while he pulled down the window shade. She could hear from the Realtor at any moment about her counter. If it were accepted, she'd have to put the furniture she was keeping and the piano into storage. She could pay for that out of the money from the house. Still, it would be another monthly bill.

They held each other. He wasn't rushing, and she was relieved. She could get aroused if Devon went slowly and she stopped thinking. She could pretend until, hopefully, she felt something.

After her counter had been accepted, when the sale of her mother's home was in escrow, Myrna went to visit Ann. The cemetery was a half-hour drive, and Myrna took her mother's car, now her car. It was still parked at Ann's, but Devon said after the sale they could garage it near their apartment. He was uncoiling from the ball of mistrust he'd become when she'd told him the house had been sold. He'd looked at her with disbelief, saying, "You had all this negotiating going on, and you forgot to mention it?"

"No, I didn't say that. I just didn't mention it then, and I am now."

"So, on purpose, you said nothing to me?" he continued, like an attorney on television.

"I didn't tell anyone. I just did it on my own."

"Oh, now I fall into the 'anyone' category—when did that happen?" After that, they hadn't talked for days. Myrna felt like two people, one who found the silence appealing and the other, who didn't want to hurt her boyfriend. On the fourth day, she gave him his favorite candy, a box of milk chocolate pecan turtles and a card that pictured a jowly puppy with sorrowful eyes. The inside was blank, and Myrna had written, "What I meant was I didn't tell anyone, not *even* you. I hope you understand. Love, M."

"I need to talk to you," Myrna said, placing tulips beside Ann's gravestone. "Are you mad that I sold the house? I don't think you are." She waited and looked at the flowers. "Well, maybe you're not in the mood to talk, so I'll keep going. I don't know what to do anymore. I've been watching Devon—you know this—and he's really an OK person. I just don't know exactly what I'm doing with him or what I'd be doing without him. I'm lost, Mom." It was too quiet. She wanted her mother's voice to corral her. She needed to hear it from her mother's throat. "This is not nearly enough, Mom," she said, starting to cry, stroking the gravestone. "It will never be enough."

When she got home, Devon was sitting on the couch with Pearl on his lap, the towel near them on the floor. Myrna walked over, grabbed Pearl and the towel, and went into the bedroom.

"Hey, what's with you?" Devon called out. "Can't I play with your toys? I play with you!" She examined Pearl. Nothing was wrong. She covered her and put her back. She was shaking as she entered the living room.

"Don't you ever take something of mine again without asking me." She didn't sound like herself.

"Wow, hold it. I thought still having one of your dollies was cute, but you're acting like a wacko. What is with you?"

"I don't know," she said, somewhat calmer. "That's the truth. I don't know what's with me, but seeing you with Pearl just made me want to claim her as mine."

"I think that's petty, that yours-and-mine stuff. I don't want your dumb doll, and you know it. I don't want any of your stuff, but I didn't think that was so important anyhow." She didn't either.

"It's not really about things, Devon. It's about me being separate from us. It's hard to explain."

"That's the polite way of saying you want to be separate from me—that's what you're really driving at, isn't it?"

"I don't know for sure if that's what I'm trying to say. I'm sorry to be vague. I'm not clear on it." She felt drowsy. She wanted her bed. Their bed, she reminded herself.

He got up, saying, "I'm going out for a walk and to think about what you don't know."

She stretched herself onto the bed over the quilt and closed her eyes. She wanted to be peaceful for a while. She felt badly thinking of Devon's hurt face, but her truth had caused him pain, not her. She wasn't trying to make him feel bad, but she was on to something about herself that she needed to understand. Maybe that was what her mother meant. They'd never really discussed living together. Devon's sublet was up, and he'd just assumed he could stay with her indefinitely. She guessed she could have said no, although at the time she didn't feel like she had that option without being a bitch that didn't care if her boyfriend had a roof over his head. Why was the roof over his head her responsibility? That sounded bitchy in her mind. Maybe she was more of a bitch than she'd ever realized. Was it really being a bitch for her to think like this? She fell asleep.

Much later, she awoke. Devon was sleeping beside her, his back to her. It was still dark, and she tried to go back to sleep. As the dawn broke, she got up and went to make coffee.

She sat on the couch with her mug and waited for Devon to get up. It was Saturday, and they had planned to spend some time at her mother's packing up things she was keeping. She wasn't thinking about that plan though. She was remembering how she and Devon met. She'd liked him, thought he was cute and easy to talk to, but she wasn't the dying-for-a-man type and had not even responded right away to his advances because she hadn't been on a flirtatious wavelength to begin with. She'd been at the park with her friend Jill's dog. Jill was away, and Myrna was dog sitting. She'd thrown a tennis ball for

Spike, but it had gone way over his head and across the field, and Devon had caught it and brought it back.

She had told him where she worked that day in the park, and a week later he showed up. At first, she thought he needed flowers or a plant, but then he got awkward and said he'd just wanted to see her and could they get together.

Her stomach tightened as she heard Devon get out of bed. She got up and poured him a cup of coffee and refilled hers. She wasn't sure he was up for good but got ready just in case. He came into the living room and sat down next to her. He reached for the coffee.

"Morning. Thanks for the java. How long have you been up?"

"A while, since it got light."

"What are we doing, Myrna? What's happening here?"

"I'm not sure—that's still the truth. I'm sorry if I upset you. I wasn't trying to, but I do feel confused about what I'm doing. Like living together, it sort of just happened out of circumstances. It wasn't something we planned to do."

"Hey, I'll move out today if that's what you want."

"I don't know if that's what I want—I mean I was glad to see you next to me when I woke up."

"You were?"

"Yeah, I was. But when you left yesterday, I was relieved to be by myself. So that's where it is for me. It's both."

"Well, I don't know if 'both' works for me. I moved in because I wanted to live with you. I had a place before I met you and could have gotten another one—it wasn't out of convenience for me if that's what you think."

"You never said that that way. I appreciate it. I did feel kind of moved in on, like I had no choice in the matter."

"Well, you do. So what do you want now?" Where was her mother? Not in her mind right then.

"I don't know what I want, Devon. Or what I don't want. I feel empty, like a sketch of a person with nothing colored in." Her eyes filled with tears. Her arms hung at her side. She didn't feel like they were hers. She looked away from him as she started to cry. He pulled her toward him. Terrified, she let him hold her. Stiff at first, crying more to herself, she slowly, one piece of her by one piece, began to relax into the consoling cave of his arms. Her crying became sobbing, grief-stricken moans she had not known were inside her. Her mother had said Devon was not for her, and maybe that was true. But in this moment, having his comfort and possibly his love seemed all she would ever need.

Caracole

Shel watched smoke from neighboring chimneys get lost in the pallid sky. He'd been staring through the back porch window for hours. He sat in the chair he and Lydia used to fight over because it felt "just right," like Goldilocks said in the story.

It had a bamboo frame that held two square cushions, one the seat and the other the back. They were zipped into green slipcovers that had to be washed in cold water and dried on towels so they wouldn't shrink.

Looking at the trees beyond the yard, he thought about Lydia and what she'd said to him the last time they'd spoken. He'd called to give her his new phone number and to hear her.

"You're going to be fine, Sheldon, really. We both are. It is scary after so long, but like John said in our sessions, living in a rut is not being alive." She'd stressed the last word so it sounded like "a-lie-yav."

"I was fine, Lydia, so don't give me a pep talk. I can read a self-help book for lines like that," he'd said, gripping the phone. Was she sitting or standing, dressed in one of her sweater and pants sets, or wrapped in a terrycloth robe after a Vitabath? Had she already put lotion all over her body?

"Look, we've made our decision. Let's try to stay on good terms, at least for Paul's sake, OK?" She'd sighed, or had she started smoking again?

It had been their mutual decision to separate after twenty-four years of marriage, although Shel hadn't agreed at first. So now I get to be "a-lie-yav," he thought, turning off the porch light. He missed Lydia, even when he slept. His friend Chuck thought he should sell the cabin, but Shel still wanted to go there. Chuck was dating Marge, who had a friend they wanted Shel to meet. Shel wasn't ready to talk to another woman.

He put logs he'd chopped on the grate. "The thing about us," he said to the hearth, "was we were a fit, like skin and bones. Now I'm a skeleton. Happy Halloween." He laughed and imagined her giggling too. Once, their laughter had rolled into corners, and when it started not to, Shel hadn't noticed. John, the marriage counselor, said he'd gotten "too comfortable." Shel had said, "I thought that was the point."

The cabin was his getaway from his New York rental. Four months ago, he'd moved out of the co-op he'd shared with Lydia for eighteen years. He'd brought the boxes filled with the remains of his life into the newly painted living room of his "bachelor pad" and left for three tear-blurred days in the country. He hadn't wept since his father's death eight years before, but then he'd cried next to Lydia in their still-vital bed.

He made a fire he could inhabit. After it burned, he took the leftover half of a turkey sandwich he'd brought from the city and ate standing in the kitchen.

"Good night, baby," he whispered later, nestling into his pillow.

Returning to New York the following afternoon, Shel was surprised to find Paul sitting in the living room. He had a set of keys but usually phoned ahead of a visit. He seemed unraveled.

"What's wrong, son?"

"Dad, I got something to tell you." He motioned to the chair next to the couch, and Shel came and sat in it.

"Mom's moving in with that guy she's been seeing, the dentist."

"They just met, what, a month or so ago?"

"Yeah, I know, but that's why I even told you right off about him, because they sort of clicked, and I didn't want you to get caught off guard."

"What about the apartment?"

"Mom's selling it—planned to anyhow, I think sooner as opposed to later." Lydia had gotten the apartment, Shel the cabin. The apartment was worth a lot more, but their lawyers had figured that into their final settlement.

"Where does he live?" Shel asked flatly.

"In Westchester, but I can't remember which town—Larchmont, maybe. He's got a big home from when he and his wife raised their kids. He's a widower."

"You were smart to move out when you did, huh?" Shel said, attempting a grin.

Paul reached over, putting his hand on his father's arm.

"Dad, I know this is a shocker."

They ordered Chinese food and watched a football game. When it finished, Paul went home. Shel loaded and started the dishwasher, set the coffeemaker for 6:45 a.m., and grabbed a towel from the linen closet. It was beige and part of the set he'd hurriedly bought at a bath shop on Broadway.

"What are your colors in the bathroom?" the sales lady had sprightly asked.

"Just neutral kind," he'd answered, not recalling that room at all.

He undressed in the bedroom, putting some clothing away and bringing the rest into the bathroom to place in the hamper. He stood nude in front of the medicine chest mirror. His face was flushed from the country air. He looked through his tired eyes. He would be fifty in February. Thanksgiving was in a month. Lydia had a new man whose wife loved him until she died. Some men have that effect on women, Shel thought, searching his uncombed hair.

An early November snowfall at the cabin sealed the leaves for mulching. He took spirited walks in clammy wind, trying to banish fantasies of Lydia enjoying her new lover. Shel's legs mashed the snow as each image turned his head.

Chuck and Marge invited Shel for Thanksgiving dinner, and he took Paul out on Christmas. Shel spent New Year's Eve in his apartment with a fine bottle of cabernet he decided he could afford and lasagna from a gourmet takeout market. He watched Dick Clark live from Times Square, hardly believing it would be 1999, the last year before the new millennium. He thought about years before, how worried he and Lydia had been when Paul insisted on going to Times Square with a group of friends from high school. Shel tried to recall what he and Lydia had done once Paul left with his friends and his parents' cautions.

They went to Sheila and Ronald's for dinner, he remembered. Their son, Henry, was with Paul, and they'd watched the ball drop on television, sipping champagne and absurdly looking for the boys in the crowd. He and Lydia must have kissed at midnight. Why couldn't he remember distinctly? When had they stopped kissing?

He turned off the television even though it wasn't midnight quite yet. He poured himself more cabernet. He was maybe going to drink the entire bottle.

"That's a good boy—here's your treat, Otis." Shel patted his new roommate's head. They'd been out for a walk, and Otis had fully relieved himself. He was perfectly housebroken; one advantage of Shel's decision to choose an adult dog. Otis had chosen him, too, the instant Shel peered into the cage at the ASPCA. Facing front, Otis had stared expectantly at Shel as if he'd taken too long to come and had better hurry up and bring him home.

It was Paul's idea. Shel hadn't been that receptive at first, but then spring came and he figured a dog would force him out of doors even if he were feeling low.

Otis rested a lot, and Shel was grateful. He knew some dogs were hyperactive (he'd shared the elevator with them), but Otis had a calm to be envied. His favorite spot was near the window in a corner of the living room where he settled. Shel tossed him a rawhide chew bone saying, "Now that you have a treat, I'm having a beer." It was Friday, and they were staying in the city because Shel had a date Saturday night. Some kind of déjà vu had been occurring ever since he'd confirmed the plan. Songs from when Shel was a teen kept popping out of his mouth.

"'Another Saturday night, and I ain't got nobody. I got some money 'cause I just got paid,'" he sang, pouring himself a Bud Light. He felt like the awkward adolescent he'd been, standing on one side of the gym at a dance, enjoying the music, but afraid to make the kind of moves the guys who were operators did. He had a girlfriend toward the end of high school, but he graduated a year ahead of her. Lydia was the sister of one of Shel's college friends, and Shel met her at the friend's wedding. She seemed vulnerable, not knowing a lot of the guests of her brother's, who were a few years older than she was, so Shel introduced himself to her at the reception. Later he asked her to dance, and holding her, he felt home.

"Saturday night is kind of intimidating," he had said to Chuck a week ago.

"Thing is, Helen's got a young daughter and a busy job, so she likes to spend nights home with her, but the kid's with her dad every other weekend.

What's the real difference, Shels? It's just gonna be a quiet dinner at Marge's apartment, very informal."

He put his beer and newspaper on the coffee table, and went into the bedroom for his reading glasses. Noticing the blinking red light on his phone's answering machine, he hit "play" and heard an unfamiliar voice saying, "Hi, Shel, this is Helen Gaines, Marge's friend, and we're going to meet tomorrow evening for dinner, but I'd appreciate hearing from you tonight if you get this," and she gave her number. He grabbed a pen and jotted it down, replaying the message to make sure he'd gotten it right.

"Well, boy, what do I do now?" he said to Otis, who had followed him in. He retrieved his drink and swallowed.

"Here goes, Otis," he said, and dialed.

"Hello?"

"Is this Helen?"

"Yes."

"Hi, this is Shel Burnham, calling you back. Am I catching you at a good time?"

"Yes, thanks. I got your number from information, and I just wanted to introduce myself over the phone, before this dinner tomorrow night, where we'll have four eyes watching us to see how we're doing with each other." Her voice reminded him of someone's, maybe an actress's whose name wasn't coming to him.

"Yeah, I know what you mean. I haven't dated since, well, for a very long time, and I'm way rusty at the whole process, but I'm looking forward to meeting you."

"And I feel likewise. I have been dating some over the past two years, so I've had time to break it in a bit." He wondered what she looked like.

"That's an interesting way to put it." He waited, but she said nothing. "Chuck says you have a daughter?"

"Sure do. Beth. She's ten years old. Have you any kids?"

"One son, Paul; he just turned twenty-two. He's my best friend."

"I hope someday I can say that about Beth, but I've got mothering a teenager still ahead of me." She laughed lightly. Otis, having heard something outside, started barking.

"Quiet, boy," Shel commanded, adding, "Sorry about that. I'm learning how to live with a dog."

"What kind do you have?"

"He's a mixture, part beagle. He's just been with me a few weeks, but it seems longer." Otis left the bedroom to investigate.

"Beth begged for a pet when she was smaller, so I got her a bird. He's more mine than hers, and she still wants a dog."

"It's a little like being a parent, being responsible for another life." He looked at the clock radio. It was 7:30 p.m., and he was starving. He'd eaten an early lunch at the office.

"That's one of the reasons I've stood my ground with Beth, but there are times when I would like a good watchdog."

"He's definitely that; plus, I love coming home to his utter enthusiasm. I tell him, 'You just saw me this morning! What's the big deal?' but he acts like we're having a major reunion." She laughed again, a feathery note that danced in his ear. "Have you had dinner?" he asked, stunning himself.

"No, I haven't."

"Neither have I. Um, would you want to have a bite tonight, kind of a sneak preview date?"

"I think I'd like to, but I do have one condition."

"And what might that be?"

"Let's keep it a secret. You know, not tell Chuck and Marge tomorrow night. Does that sound OK to you?"

"Sure does," he said, starting to tremble. "So, tell me where I'm going." She gave her address, and they agreed to meet in an hour.

After dressing, Shel evaluated his effort. He wore fitted blue jeans, an ivory turtleneck, and a burgundy sweater. He wondered if he was handsome. He thought his body was presentable—he'd been working out at the gym for that—but his face was so known to him, he couldn't tell how a stranger would see it. He smiled into the mirror on the back of his bedroom door. It was an improvement, but he'd look idiotic forcing it. He went into the living room, and Otis looked up from his rawhide bone.

"So, buddy, do I make the cut?"

He took a crosstown bus and arrived exactly one hour after he and Helen had hung up. He gave the doorman her name, and within moments, an attractive woman was walking toward him.

"Hi, I'm Helen." She smelled faintly of some perfume or soap that made him realize he'd forgotten about cologne. "There's a homey place around the corner with great burgers and salads. Want to try it?"

They were seated and ordered glasses of chardonnay. When the drinks came, Shel raised his glass to hers, saying "cheers" and then taking more than a sip.

"It's nice to be out. Thanks for coming over," she said. "A lot when Beth is gone for the weekend, I sort of hibernate."

"Being alone has its good and bad aspects. I've been learning about both," he said, and swallowed more wine. She was easier to talk to on the phone, he thought. Now, he felt on the spot to be interesting, which he doubted he was. "How long have you known Marge?"

"Since we were little. Grew up on the same block. After high school we lost touch for about ten years, and then one day my mom called to say Marge had written to her asking how to contact me. We met for lunch, and that was it. She's one of my closest friends. Is Chuck one of yours?"

"Well, yes, he is, or has come to be. We work together, and when I started having marital problems, he tried to help."

"Divorce is rough, even when it's for the best. You definitely need support. How did your son take it?"

"Hard at first. Now he kind of fathers me and mothers his mom." He hoped that didn't sound strange. "How about your daughter?"

"She was eight and very attached to her dad; she still is, and he's a good father…" She stopped abruptly and took up her glass. He didn't want to ask about her ex-husband, which seemed too personal. He couldn't think of one thing to say next.

"What's your dog's name?"

"Otis. It was already his name when I got him from the ASPCA. It fits him too. Did you ever have a dog?"

"When I was a kid, we had a cocker spaniel, but I was more interested in horses and took riding lessons. I haven't been on a horse in years, but I sure loved it then."

"Does your daughter ride?"

"No, but she loves sports—soccer, softball, bike riding. We ride our bikes together in the park."

When the bill came, Helen took her purse while he said, "No, please let me take care of this. I'm not trying to be macho, but I was brought up a little shy of our present times."

"Thank you, Shel. I didn't expect it but fine. My turn next time."

He walked Helen back to her lobby.

"We don't have to pretend tomorrow night if you don't want to," she said. "We could tell them the truth."

"And miss the fun of watching them watch us?" he said playfully.

She smiled, saying, "All right then. I will follow your lead."

He took a window seat in a nearly empty bus, relieved to be going home. He'd had a few rough moments talking to Helen, but he'd managed. He liked her—not in the youthful, lusty way he'd liked Lydia. He'd worked hard then, pushed himself to win her attention. Lydia had phoned a few days before, needing some tax information from the previous year. At the end of the call, she'd said, "Oh, and congrats on the puppy. Paul says he's adorable."

His stop was next. Otis was waiting for him, missing him. They would take a long walk even though it was late.

An Early Start

It was difficult for her to wait for Pietro while the wind pierced her skin with frozen needles. Moving quickly gave her comfort, but Pietro was small, probably five years old. Bellina wasn't sure, but she knew her tenth birthday was April 6.

The narrow streets that scrambled north from the river were empty. They had gotten an early start, before Luigio awoke. Bellina stayed close to the curb, watching ahead and behind. Pietro hopped or skipped, then ran to catch up as if it were a game.

"Luigio can't yell at us now," he chanted.

"No, not this morning, but we better have a good day, or…"

"Or can we stay in the train station, Lina?" Pietro had jumped in front of her and was walking backward.

"Maybe just one night, or we'll get put in jail," she said, turning him frontward.

"Are we going to the Duomo?"

"Of course, Pietro, now hurry."

The dome of the cathedral seemed to give the sky its melon hue as they approached the Piazza del Duomo from the west.

"My turn first," Pietro said, running toward the east door of the baptistery, which stood just yards from the cathedral. He studied the ten bronze panels of the door.

"That man's tired because he had to work while everyone else got to play," he said, pointing to the drunken Noah slumped on the ground. Bellina half listened to her brother's story and tried to warm herself by pulling the shreds of green sweater more tightly around her. Pigeons hungrily crossed the piazza from all sides, ready for the throwers who arrived each day, as if to Mecca, waving arms that sprayed bread bits, crumbs, and crackers into the square. Bellina and Pietro, hands open, walked among the feeders saying, "Please, for us some, too, please."

Bellina deftly scanned the faces of the women passing by.

"Is Mama here?" asked Pietro, also looking around.

"No," she murmured.

"Maybe she's never coming back; maybe she got eaten by a monster; maybe…"

"Pietro, shut up! There's no such thing as monsters."

"Why is it taking so long then?"

"It just is. Now we have to work hard today."

They began on the long, wide Via dei Cerchi, whose elegant stores were about to open. Her mother called them "fancy-lady shops."

"Florence has leather everything—shoes, purses, wallets, belts—it's what they make here for the people that can pay. But smelling it is free," she would say.

They walked with one hand each outstretched while Bellina repeated, "Signora, signore, something for us, please," faintly melancholy, the way her mother had done. The perfumed women and men wearing cashmere coats were usually generous, and by midday, Bellina and Pietro had enough lire to satisfy Luigio. They had a few extra coins for two apples. Bellina ate hers slowly; it was her favorite fruit. She was excited now about the money she hoped they'd make after lunch. She would hide it somewhere and add to it whenever she could. If Mama doesn't come back soon, she thought, we will run away from Luigio and find her. Pietro reached for the burlap satchel containing their earnings.

"How much did we make so far?" he asked.

"Not that much."

"But it looks like lots."

"Well, it isn't, and we'll have to work harder the rest of today. In fact, we'll split up in San Lorenzo so we can cover the whole market place," Bellina said with finality. Pietro sensed without understanding that his sister had kept something from him.

Teresa tried to nurse her infant, but he squirmed away.

"Come, Pietro," she whispered while the baby wailed.

"Lina, bring the juice bottle right away," Teresa said, glancing at Luigio asleep on the cot that served as their couch. The juice calmed Pietro, and Teresa reluctantly considered giving him milk from the bottle too. Bellina stood close so she could help wipe Pietro's dribbling. Luigio groaned. He'll sleep awhile longer, Teresa thought, holding Pietro closer. It is truly God's doing that I can have this precious son from such a good-for-nothing—good for this at least, she thought. He doesn't even believe the boy is his. Why should he? He's half drunk when we make love, barely able to do it or remember. When she'd told him she was pregnant, he had hit her, shouting, "You been laying with Roberto again—wasn't one kid with him enough?" Later, she had offered to swear on the cross that the baby was his.

"That's just a piece of metal to a hussy like you. I told you, I can't have children or by now I would have some." She gave up trying to convince him, and Luigio remained indifferent to her growing stomach. When Pietro was born, Luigio gave him one serious look and decided that he'd been right all along.

"Now there are two of Roberto's children to feed, and work is hard to find."

"We will earn our share, just as Lina and I have."

Pietro fussed in her arms. She guided his thumb into his mouth, glad that her thoughts had been interrupted. She gently shook him to calm him and herself. When he was asleep, she rose and put him in the laundry basket that was his bed and placed it near the heater. Bellina watched, her brown eyes open as if she never blinked.

When Pietro was four months old, they started to work again. In the four years that passed, Teresa honed her routine of taking the children to beg with her. Bellina was especially smart at it, and Pietro tagged along, encouraging contributions just by his presence. Luigio worked on and off. Teresa began thinking about leaving him and going to live with her sister, Rosa, in Bari. A lady she knew in the straw market had written a letter to Rosa for her and had promised to mail it.

A week before Pietro's fifth birthday, Teresa put the children to bed and left for a quick trip to the train station to ask about the schedule and cost to go to Bari. She could make it there and back before Luigio got home. She didn't want the children to know her plan until they could go.

The moonless night was silent. Teresa clutched her purse though all it contained was the key to her home. The darkness made it hard for her to recognize the streets. She became unsure of where she was. She saw light at the end of a long, unfamiliar street. Many steps to entranceways jutted out at unexpected points on the slender sidewalk, so Teresa, afraid of tripping, went into the curb. Suddenly, the light she was walking toward gleaned from behind her as well. She heard only seconds of the car's revving as it bumped her to one side without stopping.

The bells of Santa Maria Novella peeled five times above the clamor of the motorbikes that zipped around the city. The Arno flowed west unhurried, like a teal thread sewn into the Tuscan landscape. They took the Lungarno home, and Pietro looked for boats. When they arrived, Luigio snatched the satchel from Bellina and dumped its contents on his bed.

"Well, well, not bad. Maybe we're lucky your mother, the slut, took off with one of her tomcats!" He packed the money into his wallet and left. He had recently started another job.

Bellina went into the bathroom and removed her right sock and retrieved a neatly folded roll of lire from it. She wrapped toilet paper around it and wedged it between the radiator, which never worked, and the wall. She planned to check it often and to add to it.

Their earnings slowed over the next week, and Bellina was not able to save much. She took Pietro to the straw market since they hadn't worked there for a while. A group of American tourists who said, "*Buongiorno*, bambinos" offered them cookies as well as some lire. They passed a stand operated by Marni, a friend of their mother's. Seeing them, she jumped up from her folding chair and came around her display of hats and bags.

"Bellina, Pietro, hello. I have not seen you in so long, and where is your mother? I have something for her," she said, looking over their heads.

"Mama's gone, and we don't know where and…"

"Hush now. My brother doesn't understand that our mother will return, um, soon," Bellina said, staring at Marni's shoes.

"Well, here's something for her that I've been holding." Marni handed Bellina a letter. "It's from her sister, your aunt Rosa, who lives in Bari."

"Did Mama go to see Aunt Rosa?" Pietro asked.

"She was thinking of going but waiting to hear back first—at least that's what I thought she intended to do," Marni said.

"What does this letter say? Please, I cannot read yet," Bellina said, ripping it open.

Marni hesitated, then read it quickly to herself and then aloud: "'Dear Teresa, it was good to hear from you. Of course you and the children are welcome to come here and stay with us until you find your own place. Gino and I await your plans. Come sooner, not later. Love, Rosa.'" Marni omitted the sentence "It's time you left that awful man you live with."

"That's where she is—she went ahead to make it better for us," Bellina said joyfully. "We must go there. Will you help us?"

"I will if I can, but what about…?"

"Luigio? He is not our real father—even he says so. He's out of the house a lot right now working, so we have to leave right away. He always loses his job." Bellina wanted to tell Marni about her extra money and whispered it so Pietro wouldn't hear. He was trying on some of Marni's straw hats, piling one after the other on his disappearing head.

"All right then. Can you and your brother get out early tomorrow morning and meet me at the train station? I will buy you tickets to Bari and give you a note for your mother." Bellina nodded, more thrilled than she could ever remember.

That evening, they packed sparingly so as not to alert Luigio. They left just before seven and departed on the 8:15 a.m. going to Faenza, only two hours away, where they would change trains and spend another nine hours traveling south to Bari. Marni waved to them as the train pulled away from the platform.

"Is this the biggest train in the world, Lina?"

"I think it must be one of the very biggest," Bellina said, keeping her promise to herself to always answer Pietro in some way even if her thoughts were elsewhere.

Pietro fell asleep on the way to Bari, the last stop for the train. Bellina stayed awake, eyes closed, picturing her mother's face surprised and glad to see them. Arriving at Bari, Bellina asked the ticket man for directions, showing him the address Marni had written down for them. It was close, and within minutes she and Pietro were knocking on the door.

"Who is there?" a woman asked.

"It's Bellina and Pietro. Aunt Rosa?"

The light from within caused the children to squint as they entered.

"It is you. My goodness, that was fast." Their aunt looked outside, having left the door ajar. "Teresa?" she called into the chilled air. Bellina was confused.

"Mama is here already, isn't she?"

"Your mother—no, she's not here—she didn't come with you? You came by yourselves? I don't understand this." Bellina stood in the middle of the room holding herself with her bony arms and began to cry. So did Pietro, because he rarely saw her cry.

"Come now. Sit down and tell me what has happened to you," said Aunt Rosa, leading them inside.

"One morning, Pietro and I woke up, and Mama wasn't there. We thought she'd gone out for milk or something and waited, but she never came back. We looked for her at the Duomo and all around the marketplace, but we couldn't find her. We saw Marni, who gave us your letter, so we came here, but we thought Mama had come here too."

"Luigio says Mama went away with a man named Tom Cat," Pietro volunteered.

"Pietro doesn't know what he's saying. Mama isn't with another man," Bellina said assuredly.

"No, of course not," Rosa said. "She wanted to come here with you both. Uncle Gino is a policeman. He's at work right now, but when he gets home, he'll call the police in Florence, and they will find your mother." Rosa kept quiet about her fears.

The children slept on the couch, their heads at opposite ends, warmed by a blue quilt. Bellina awoke to the sound of her uncle on the telephone.

"Teresa Brizzi. Yes, she's medium size, about five five, a hundred and thirty-five pounds. No, not married, but she lives with Luigio Pascoli. But he's not looking for her. I am. She's my sister-in-law, and my wife is worried because she left home sometime over the past month and never came back." Gino listened for a moment and then covered the mouth piece. "Rosa, does your sister have any birthmarks, scars, anything noticeable like that?" Rosa shook her head no.

"She has a tooth missing. When she smiles, you can see it," Bellina said. Gino spoke this information into the phone and hung up.

The telephone call came in the morning eight days later. Gino wrote down the information, saying, "Sounds like her for sure. Thanks so much" before he hung up.

"What is it?" Rosa asked excitedly. The children were outside playing.

"Your sister—at least I believe it's Teresa—is in a hospital in Florence. She was struck by a car—hit-and-run, the creep. She has a fractured skull, has been unconscious most of the time and delirious when she is conscious. Couldn't tell them her name but did call for 'Lina and Pietro' a few times. Came in with nothing on her but a house key."

Rosa and the children went to Florence the next day. Bellina was fearful of somehow seeing Luigio. Aunt Rosa said he couldn't hurt them, even if he found out what had happened. The hospital was in a neighborhood she didn't know. Her aunt talked to a nurse at the reception desk for a long time. Bellina began to worry that her mother was not, after all, there. She steadied herself just in case. Finally, another nurse led them to an elevator, then down a hallway into a room with four beds. Bellina was first to see her mother asleep in the bed near the back wall.

"Mama," she said, rushing toward the bed. The nurse followed and took her shoulders.

"Your mother may not wake up, but you can try to talk to her."

"Mama, it's me, Lina. Are you tired? It's OK. You can rest. Pietro and Aunt Rosa are here too. We live in Bari with her, and you will, too, as soon as you get better!" Teresa's eyes fluttered, and she mumbled something.

"I think she heard you," said the nurse. "That's good."

Pietro and Aunt Rosa stood by the bed on the other side.

"It's really Mama," he said, a bit amazed. "I rode on a big train all night," he told his mother. They stayed there for over an hour, but Teresa did not awake.

In the reception area again, they met with the doctor who was treating her.

"I am so happy to find out who this poor woman is. She was not in good shape at first, but she's improving. We expect her to recover."

"When can she come home?" Bellina asked.

"Probably not for a month or more, but your coming to see her will help her to get better faster."

Aunt Rosa decided they would stay for one week in a pension near the hospital. The next day when they visited, Teresa did not awake, although she seemed to stir again when they spoke to her. Then on the afternoon of their third day, her eyes were open when they approached her bed.

"Mama, it's me, Lina. We are here with you." Teresa seemed to be listening. She looked in Bellina's direction. It was a start.

By the time they had to leave for Bari, Teresa was conscious much of the time.

It was two weeks before Christmas, and the crisp air smelled of pine and burning wood. Uncle Gino took the children to pick out a tree. Pietro wanted a huge one.

"My boy, we must live in the house, too, not just the tree!" Gino said, steering him toward a more manageable one.

"I don't care how big or small the tree is," said Bellina, "but can we put a beautiful star on the top?"

In the days that followed, Bellina helped her aunt clean the house and bake holiday treats. It kept her busy, but that was all. She missed working. She hadn't earned a coin since she'd arrived, except for an allowance Aunt Rosa gave to her and Pietro, but that wasn't the same.

On the day before Christmas, her aunt prepared a turkey. Bellina chopped celery, olives, and onions for the stuffing.

"You look bored, Bellina, but after the holidays, then you will be busy." Bellina's eyes brightened.

"Will I be able to work then, Aunt Rosa?"

"Well, yes, homework. You and Pietro are going to school."

"School! I've never been to school, and Mama never said I had to go. When she comes back, we're going to work again. I'm not going to school!"

"I talked to your mother at the hospital, and she said if we didn't need you to work, she would love for you and Pietro to start school. You're going to learn to read and write. You can't get along without that anymore." Bellina chopped intensely. Her mother had always gotten along without school. Maybe Aunt Rosa hadn't really talked to Teresa about it.

The next day, Christmas, they called the hospital, and when Bellina said again that she wouldn't go to school, her mother said, "Lina, you must go. It will be good for you and Pietro. Maybe I can learn to read too." She sounded so hopeful that Bellina kept quiet. She felt trapped. She wanted to run away, but she didn't know where to go. She didn't want to leave when her mother was about to join them. She decided to pretend to go to school but to work instead.

On the first day, her aunt took them so Bellina had to enter the four-story brick building. She had never seen so many children at one time. They were various ages and chattered about their holidays to one another. Bellina felt nauseous and took a drink of water at the fountain. A girl about the same age came up behind her.

"Are you new?" she asked. Bellina didn't respond.

In the registration office, the secretary, Mrs. Sensi, gave Aunt Rosa some forms to fill out, then looked at Pietro, saying, "You will be in Mr. Gilardi's class—it's kindergarten, and those children just started last September, so you're not very far behind." Pietro gave her a guarded look.

"Bellina, you will have more of an adjustment to make, and we will help you in every way that we can. You are almost ten and should be in fourth grade, but first you will meet with our placement teacher, Mr. Dicino."

He was a pudgy man with a wrinkled jacket and a mustache that weighed down his upper lip. He showed Bellina a series of pictures and asked her to make up stories about them. Thinking this silly, she answered concisely.

"You don't like to use your imagination much, do you, young lady?"

"No. It…"

"Yes? It what?"

"It seems like a waste of time," she said bluntly.

"What would you rather do?"

"Work—be outside earning money."

"I understand that you are very experienced at that, right?" She nodded, starting to blush. He placed his wallet on the desk.

"Take it," he said, "and tell me how much money I have." She quickly went through the wallet and returned it, saying, "Forty-seven thousand lire."

"Exactly right, Miss Bellina. Can you tell me what you do at work?"

About an hour later, they returned to Mrs. Sensi's office.

"This child has much knowledge," he said, "and she is uniquely proficient in mathematics. I suggest that instead of holding her back, she be placed in fourth grade with her peers. She will require daily tutoring for reading and writing."

Within minutes, Bellina was presented to the class of fifteen boys and twelve girls and to her first teacher, Ms. Graffia. The children watched as she awkwardly took her seat. Ms. Graffia explained that her needs in the classroom would be somewhat special for a while.

At recess, Bellina looked for Pietro. He was climbing the bars with some other boys. The girl from the water fountain walked toward her.

"Hi, I'm Stella. What's your name again?"

"Bellina."

"Do you always get to wear your hair loose?"

"Sure," she said, noticing Stella's neatly woven braids. "Don't you?"

"Not to school. You're lucky."

Contrary to Bellina's plan of truancy, her aunt took them to school and made it her niece's responsibility to bring Pietro home. When Teresa finally arrived from the hospital, she wanted to hear about school.

"I like it better than working," Pietro said. "There are more kids."

"What about you, Lina?"

"It's all right."

Later, when they were alone, Teresa said, "Lina, you look so sad. Is school really OK?" Bellina could feel tears coming. She forced her voice out to beat them.

"It's hard to go there. I'm not like the others. I'm more grown up. I don't need to know the dumb things they learn, and they think I'm stupid—that's what I hate the most."

"I never went to school, but if I had to start now, I would feel very out of place."

"Can't we go to work, just the two of us?"

"No. It's not like that now. I will get another kind of job, maybe at the grocery store or at the laundry. You must stay in school. I'm sorry I couldn't send you when you were smaller." Bellina took her mother's hand with both of hers and pressed it to her cheek, saying, "I guess I can stand it, Mama, now that you're back." Teresa pulled Bellina into her chest. They held each other hard and cried.

The Block

Everyone on the block called her Nana. I would see her in the mornings, sitting on a fold-up wooden chair drinking coffee from a thermos. She had a face like an apple with a big bite out of it. I was seven, and she was eightysomething.

After school, I would rush home, hoping that Nana was still there. Often she was, and my mother would let me stay with her until it started to get dark. I showed Nana all the things I could do—hopscotch, roller-skate, bike ride. She clapped and laughed, but if I fell, she would hobble toward me looking so grave that I would start crying whether I was hurt or not.

"Are you the oldest person ever?" I asked her once.

"No dear, God is the oldest person. And the youngest too."

"How can that be, Nana?"

"Because he is in all of us."

"But I thought he was in heaven."

"Well, I haven't been to heaven as yet, so I don't know if he's there too."

I hated when it rained because then Nana stayed in her apartment on the sixth floor of our building. We lived on the eighth floor.

That Halloween, I knocked on Nana's door. I was a very scary witch with a black tooth and a magic broom.

"Trick or treat, but don't be scared, it's me, Cammie."

"Yes, come in. I'd better get you a treat before you cast an awful spell on me."

I had never been inside her home. From somewhere, I heard pretty violin music. Two matching lamps with shades of rose silk and fringed hems gave a soft pink glow to the room. Nana had disappeared, but I could hear her rustling close by. Everything seemed to have been there forever in just the same way. Lace doilies, round and square, covered the surfaces of the antique furniture. I wished our house looked like this. Nana came back with a bowl of candy, and I took as much as my hand could manage.

"Can I see your room?" I asked.

She led me through a short hallway to the room where the music was playing from a Victrola. I couldn't help running toward the dresser. On it were my favorite things: miniatures. So many china figures—dogs, cats, horses, a Santa Claus, and, in the center, a host of ballerinas posing, stretching, twirling, as if inspired by the violins.

"Nana, how did you get all these things?"

"It was not so difficult. I had the time."

"I'm going to be a ballerina when I grow up."

"I said that, too, at your age, Cammie, and I danced for many years."

"You did?" I said, amazed. "Which one of these did you look like?"

"Oh, I wasn't the prima ballerina. I was in the corps, the group."

"Do you have a picture from it?" She opened the top drawer and took out some photographs.

"There I am," she said, singling out one of the faces from a cluster of white organdy.

"Nana, you're so beautiful. Are you a princess?"

"No, we are swans, and we glide around the lake. But now you had better get going, or your trick-or-treat bag won't fill up." She smiled and started to put the pictures in the drawer. One fell, and I picked it up. It was of a man with dark hair.

He wore a uniform.

"Who's this, Nana?"

"He was my husband," she said slowly. "He was killed in the First World War. He was very brave."

"Do you have children?"

"No, there wasn't time for that, but I have always had little ones, Cammie, like you." The music had stopped, and so, it seemed, had the ballerinas.

I didn't know when Nana's birthday was, but I wanted to give her a present. Around the corner was a laundry with a cat, which had just had a litter, and they were trying to give the kittens away. I wanted one for me and one for Nana. My mother said my father hated cats and Nana was too old to take care of a pet.

"Mama, please," I begged in front of everyone at the laundry. "If Nana can't take care of the kitty, I'll bring it back, promise."

"Well, all right," my mother said, looking at our audience. I picked the biggest, fattest one.

We reached the block, and I held the kitten close to me. A crowd of our neighbors had gathered right where Nana sat, and I could tell something was wrong. Someone was saying, "Call an ambulance," but Nana died before it came. I was able to get close enough to see her lying on a blanket on the ground. Her head was tilted toward me, and she seemed to be looking at me, but when I held up the kitten, her expression didn't change. Then my mother took me upstairs.

A few days later, we were told that Nana left a letter instructing that her miniatures, all of them, be given to me after she passed away.

My mother and I brought the kitten back to the laundry. The owner groaned when he saw us.

I arranged the miniatures on my dresser and put the ballerinas in the middle, but they seemed out of place, just as the block seemed to be a different street.

The Inside Edge

"Stay on your inside edge, Julie. That's better. Slightly bend the knees—yah, good," Inga called to the ten-year-old child as she glided, a bit jerkily, through the figure. Julie's ankles ached, and her toes burned from the cold.

"Arms out! Here, follow me," said Inga, gracefully sweeping in front of Julie. Now, with Inga's blades cutting in a perfect eight, Julie's skates fit the groove easily, like a train on the track.

The rink at Rockefeller Center was about a fourth filled, but it was only 9:15 a.m. Julie's father, Bob Hermann, skated amateurishly with Ron Klein, another "Sunday father."

"Julie's the curly top, huh, Bob?" asked Ron.

"Yep. She's getting pretty good at this."

"Hey, I'd get good, too, if I had a gorgeous blonde like that teaching me," said Ron.

"Inga is charming. She's Swedish, the Sonja Henie type, healthy, robust," Bob said as Ron cut him off, asking, "What are you seeing her or something?"

"As a matter of fact, yes, Ron. Now keep that to yourself. I don't want Julie hearing about it."

"Why not? You're allowed."

"Well, Julie took the divorce pretty hard. She knows I date women in general, but that's different than her skating teacher."

"I get it, Bob, OK, hush-hush." Ron grinned. "You lucky dog!"

Later, Julie sat at a table in the coffee shop that overlooked the skating rink. She, Taffy, and Pam were slurping ice-cream sodas and eating fries floating in ketchup. Taffy was the youngest but the only "pro." At eight, she skated every day for five hours. She was training for competitions all the time. Taffy had shown Julie the "bunny hop." It was the only jump Julie could do. It was much easier than it looked, so Julie showed it off whenever she wanted to impress the anonymous crowd of spectators who seemed to permanently reside at Rockefeller Plaza.

"I can do spread eagle now—did you see me before?" said Pam boastfully.

"No," said Taffy, "show me on the next session."

"No," lied Julie, who'd seen Pam doing spread eagle but would never give her the satisfaction of that. She didn't like Pam, just Taffy. Pam was stuck-up and a better skater than Julie was.

Julie saw her father coming toward her.

"Hi, pussycat, ready to go?"

"Dad, can't I skate another session?"

"Well, today I want to squeeze in a movie before we go to Grandma's. It's a Western, *The Guns of Navarone*."

"Westerns are boring," said Pam, not looking at anyone.

"Who asked you?" snapped Julie, rising.

"I like the horses," Taffy said cheerfully.

It was twenty minutes past nine; they were more than an hour late, but her mother didn't get mad, ever. As they rode up the elevator, Julie was coming down, getting quiet. Bob expected it; he, too, felt it.

"Are you gonna come in, Dad?"

"No, it's late."

"You never want to—you don't want to see Mom, right?"

"Julie, give us some time. It'll get better between us, OK?"

Julie shut the door and waited until she heard the elevator come. Then she ran to the living room window and watched her father, seven stories below, walk into the gutter and hail a cab.

She gave a perfunctory hello to her mother, who was in bed, knitting. They chatted for a while; then Julie went to her pink, dreamy, toy-filled bedroom. Unlike most girls her age, Julie had her own phone. It was the meager benefit of having a single mother, who needed a phone that would rarely be busy. As she entered her room, it was ringing.

"Hello?"

"Julie?" said a strange yet familiar voice.

"Yeah."

"Julie, this is Inga." Julie was surprised and curious. "Hi, Inga. How did you get my number?"

"From the phone book, Julie. Is your father still there?"

"No, he went home."

"Oh, how long ago?"

"I don't know, a little while," said Julie, beginning to feel unaccountably queasy. "Why?"

"Oh, well I—I didn't confirm your lesson for next week with him and—" Suddenly, Julie heard the shrill tone of a doorbell. "Julie—I must get off. I will see you next week," said Inga nervously, and hung up. Julie stared at the phone, the conversation making less and less sense to her because it wasn't what Inga had said; it was how she sounded: timid, apologetic, not at all like when she gave Julie instructions on the ice. What was so scary about her dad?

She picked up the phone and dialed her father's number to let him know Inga had called. No answer. Where was he? Julie recalled the doorbell that had cut short the call from Inga. Now Julie was trembling because she was thinking something impossible, that her dad was at Inga's apartment, not at his. Unable to figure anything out, she finally slept but not comfortably. She dreamed that Inga was giving her father a skating lesson but being shy and cautious. They were both ignoring Julie. Taffy skated up, saying, "Is your dad going to get married to Inga?" Julie awoke ahead of her alarm, remembering the dream. She dressed and went into the kitchen. Her mother, Edna, had fixed oatmeal, but Julie wasn't hungry.

"Julie, you don't look very rested this morning."

"I'm not, Mom—I had a hard time getting to sleep. Maybe it was dinner. Grandma made stuffed cabbage—kinda spicy."

"Could be. Well do you feel all right?"

"Yeah, just tired."

"Did you have a good time with your father?" Edna asked impersonally.

"Yeah."

"You're not very talkative, dear."

"Sorry, Mom, I just don't have much to say."

The following Sunday, Bob Hermann picked up Julie, and they went to the coffee shop at the rink for a quick breakfast before her lesson. Bob was on alert. His daughter was troubled; he could tell. He would wait to see if she volunteered something, but before the day was over, he would get it out of her.

They sat in a booth opposite the large window that faced the rink. Two orange vehicles were cleaning the ice.

"Dad, I gotta ask you something," Julie said, not looking at him.

"Shoot, honey."

"Did you go home Sunday after you left me?" Her question startled him, and he answered quickly, "Yes, where else would I go?"

"To Inga's," she said flatly. Bob almost winced as he looked at her round, freckled face set in coldness beyond her years.

"Honey," he started, hesitantly, "I'm not going to lie to you. I've got to be brutally frank. Inga and I have been dating, and yes, that's where I went Sunday. Does that upset you? Please, Julie, talk to me."

She remained silent, building a wall of sugar cubes. Finally she said, "Are you going to marry Inga?"

"No, absolutely not. I like her, but I'm not marrying her or anyone else for a long time. But I do go out with women, Julie. I need the companionship. You may not understand it yet, but—"

"I understand more than you think. You don't have to keep secrets from me, Dad. It's not like I want you to be all alone."

"And I don't want to have any secrets, from you of all people, Jule." He wondered how she had come to know about Inga. Did Edna know too? He would ask her later. He reached across the table and cupped her chin in his hand, saying, "You're a brave girl, you know that?"

They both began to eat.

Julie didn't know if she was brave exactly, but when she had heard Inga's voice so awkward and careful on the phone, it had rearranged things inside her. This was her skating instructor, who issued firm, no-nonsense commands to Julie on the ice. But off the ice, Inga had a crush on her dad, maybe even kissed him on the lips.

"Are you going to tell Inga that I know you two are dating?" Julie asked.

"No, honey, I would prefer not to. I don't even know how much longer I will be dating her because I'm much more of a single bachelor at this point in time and do not want a serious involvement."

"What about Inga?" Julie said, looking at her toast.

"I think she may want more from me than I can offer, so like I said, I may stop going out with her altogether."

"Won't that hurt her feelings, Dad?"

"It might—probably will—but I'd rather be honest with her, not lead her on, if you can understand what I mean. You're a bit young to be thinking about this kind of stuff, but I really don't want to lie to you."

After breakfast, Julie went on the ice for her lesson. Instead of Inga, a different teacher met her and said Inga had called in sick that day. Julie found herself relieved not to have to see Inga after that uncomfortable phone call on Sunday.

The following weekend, Julie didn't see her father, and the weekend after that he picked her up as usual and they headed to Rockefeller Center. In the taxi, her father turned to her saying, "By the way, I'm not dating Inga anymore; I told her I wasn't ready for something serious."

Julie nodded and looked out the window saying, "Is my lesson today with her?"

"I think it is, unless that's not what you want." Julie didn't know what she wanted except that all of this had caused her not to look forward to taking a lesson or ice-skating at all or seeing Taffy.

When she got on the ice, however, Inga came gliding up to her, smiling. "Julie, I missed you last weekend. How are you?"

Inga seemed so happy to see her that Julie smiled back. "I'm fine, Inga. Are you OK? You were sick a few weeks ago?"

"Yes, as good as new. Now let's see your figure eights."

Julie started to skate, feeling the comfort of them both pretending that her father was not part of their space or time. Julie could deal with life when there was pretending involved, when she looked like she was OK, when she could brace herself to persevere.

What Happened to John

At eighty-seven, John Kettering lived alone in the three-room apartment he had occupied since 1958. His wife, Bess, had died twelve years before, and John visited her grave infrequently. There were acquaintances that John said hello to in the market or drugstore and an old man in the park whom John talked to on occasion, but these people didn't even know John's name. In a way, this made what happened to John go more smoothly, although at times he wanted someone who knew him to be witness to it.

On the morning of December 16, 1980, John awoke at 6:20 a.m., about an hour earlier than usual. He arose quickly, noticing a surprising vigor, and headed for the bathroom. His legs felt steady for a change, and his breathing seemed fuller.

In the bathroom, in the glare of the fixture, John experienced a shock that could have killed him. In the mirror looking back at him was a man in his midthirties!

This is crazy, impossible, he thought. He examined his body. It was taut, and the hair on it was a rich brown. What is this? Have I died? Am I asleep? he wondered. He waited to awaken. Days passed, and nothing changed.

To make sure that he wasn't delusional, John finally went outside to the market.

He stopped to talk to a small child sitting in a shopping cart seat. The mother smiled at him.

"I've got a little one not much bigger than her," he said.

"They are a handful. Do you have just the one?" she asked.

He did this again, with another mother and child. It worked. He was passing for a man with small children. He also found that he wanted to buy lots of food—spicy things he hadn't eaten for years. He returned home and had the biggest meal he could remember. Then he smoked a cigar.

John was dying to tell someone, anyone, what had happened to him, but he was sure no one would believe him and might instead think he was a lunatic.

He figured he could at least tell Bess, so he went to the graveyard.

"Bess, it's me, John. Don't I look good? Like when we got married? Bess, this is 1980, and I'm thirty-five or so, out of nowhere. But I don't know what to do with it. Do I get a job again? Do I move, travel? And any second, I might change back." Changing back had begun to haunt him. He dreaded going to sleep. He prayed that he would stay this way, even though he thought that was selfish and unreasonable.

John met Helene in the laundromat. She asked him for change and continued to talk to him after he gave it to her. She was a warm, genuine woman in her late thirties. She was plain looking, and her dark-blond hair was pulled back in a careless ponytail.

"Don't you hate doing laundry? I sure do," she said on that first meeting.

"I try not to do it too often. I let it pile up," John said smiling.

"I've got two boys who go through clothes like Kleenex, so I call this place my office," she said with a chuckle.

She was easy to talk with, and John began to do his laundry more often. One evening a few months after, Helene said, "John, I guess this is kind of forward, but I would like to go out with you sometime, if you want to. But please, be honest with me if you don't care to."

John was startled and then pleased.

"Helene, I thought you had a husband to go with those kids, so I'm taken a bit off guard. I would like very much to go out with you, but I must tell you that I haven't been on a date in the longest time," John said.

"Were you involved with someone?" she asked.

"Yes, I'm a widower. I was married for fort—for many years."

"Oh, high school sweetheart?"

"Sort of."

Bess had been unable to have children. They had talked about adopting, but the lengthy application and screening process had discouraged them. John, not wanting to hurt Bess more than her inability already had, carefully avoided showing his own great disappointment, and after a while, they grew too old to be parents. So John felt as awkward about meeting Helene's children as he did about seeing their mother when he walked up to their front door for the first time.

"Hello, son, what's your name?" John said to the small boy who opened the door.

"Darrell."

"I'm John. I—here." He handed the child one of two packs of baseball bubble gum he'd brought.

"Is this sugarless?"

"I don't think so."

"Well, if it isn't, I can't chew it, but thanks for giving it to me. I'll get Mom." He turned and disappeared.

John stood looking into the tidy house. There was a lot of blue and yellow, bold and cheery. It was small, a home for an austere budget. Another, bigger boy sat on a club chair and manipulated a television computer game, seemingly unaware of John. But when the game finished, the boy got up and extended his hand, saying, "Hi, you're John. I'm Mike."

"Hi there," John said, stuffing the other pack of gum into his pocket. "Did you win your game?"

"I got six hundred forty-five points—that's pretty good. Do you play *Space Invaders*?"

"No, but I watch television."

"Oh," said Mike, unimpressed. He motioned to John to sit on the couch. Helene appeared, preceded by a light floral scent. Her hair was loosed and curled. In the car on the way to the restaurant, John said he liked her hair down.

"Thanks. So how do you like my boys?"

"Well, they're quite different. Mike seems mature, and Darrell, he's a sharp little tyke."

"Mike does tend to take being the oldest male at home a bit seriously," she said. "He tries to fill his father's shoes." Then she was silent.

Much later that evening, John learned that Helene's husband had been killed two years before in a small plane crash while on a business trip.

"I haven't dated much," Helene told John as they sipped coffee after dinner. "I wanted to give the kids, Mike especially, a chance to adjust. I think we're ready now for me to start seeing men."

"You mean a man," said John playfully.

Within six months, John and Helene knew that their feelings were deep and unique for each other. John didn't enjoy falling in love with Helene. He worried about where it could possibly go, about "changing back," although that fear and his prior life seemed to be fading like a vivid dream eventually does. But the memory of Bess was real. He had been a faithful husband and then widower, keeping Bess "with" him long after her death. Recently he and Helene had spent the night in a hotel when her boys were on overnights with friends. That evening enabled them to fulfill, irrevocably, their relationship, and now they were talking of marriage.

Helene set aside a Saturday to talk with her children about marrying John. They gathered in the living room after breakfast.

"Where are you gonna take us today, Mom?" Darrell asked.

"I'm not. I just want to talk to you and Mike."

"We always do that."

"Yeah, but this is a big talk," Mike said.

"It's good news, I think," Helene went on. "I want you two to listen, and then you'll have lots of time to say what you want about it." She settled in the chair opposite them. "You know that John is...my beau—and we love each other. Enough that we're talking about marriage."

"What do you talk about?" asked Darrell.

"They want to do it, get married to each other," said Mike irritably. "I like John, Mom, but I don't want you married, and I don't want him to live here."

"Mike, why?"

"I don't know exactly. I just don't want you and him…" He stopped and looked away.

"Mike, I'm alive and young. Did you think I'd be a widow for the rest of my life?"

"Why can't Mom get married if she wants to, Mike?" said Darrell. "We're going to grow up and get married and leave her."

"Not for a while—ages for you," Mike said.

"Yeah, but she'll be old then, and not a lot of men will want to marry her," Darrell said with concern.

"Thanks a whole bunch, Darrell." Helene felt she had lost the ball. "You guys, I love John, and he loves me. That's the main ingredient."

"What about Dad?"

"What about him, Mike?"

"Just that…that he's still our dad forever. I don't want anyone else to be my dad."

"John isn't going to take Dad's place. He's interested in being a stepparent, but he knows how much you loved your father."

"That's easy to say while he's your boyfriend—comes over and leaves. But what about when he's your husband, when this is his home too? I know a guy at school—his parents split up, and now he's got a stepfather who's always giving him orders, curfews, a hard time. Forget it."

"Who's that?" asked Darrell.

"Never mind. You're going to marry him—right, Mom?—whatever we say about it. Right?"

"I think so, Mike. But I'd rather know that you're for it."

"I like him. He can come live here," said Darrell.

"Thanks, honey." She knew Mike would need more time.

Sixteen months after their initial meeting, John and Helene were married. John claimed to be thirty-six, and Helene was thirty-eight. John had gotten used to being careful not to say things that would require his being older, but no one was watching him or expecting him to slip anyhow.

Their life together was routine but not at all dull. John worked in the accounting department of an insurance company, and Helene taught elementary school, where Darrell attended. Mike was in high school and absorbed with basketball, his studies, and girls. He found John to be a lot less threatening and was beginning to feel genuinely glad for his mother, who had not seemed so content in years.

For their first anniversary, John and Helene decided to take a cabin in the mountains for the weekend. Mike asked if he could bring a friend, Robert, someone new in the tenth grade who was on Mike's basketball team.

"We want it to be just the four of us," Helene said.

"But, Mom, the game is on Monday afternoon, and we need time to work out our stuff. We promised the coach. Each game a different pair of guys gets to plan out the strategy. Robert and I are it for Monday."

John said, "Well, in that case, you can bring your friend—OK with you, honey?"

Helene nodded, grateful that John understood.

They arrived late Friday night after a winding, spooky drive. A sprinkling of snow was on the ground, and they hoped to see more fall. Mike and Robert took the living room with the sofa bed. It was chilly, and they lit their first fire right away. Darrell had slept during most of the drive, so he had a second wind and wanted to make s'mores, toasted marshmallows with chocolate between two graham crackers, which sounded great to all of them.

"But no scary stories tonight, 'cause I got to sleep by myself far away upstairs in that room at the end of the hall," said Darrell.

"Could he camp out down here with us?" Robert said quietly to Mike, who shot him an "are you nuts?" look.

"Nah, he's little, goes to bed earlier—plus he's a noisy sleeper."

In the morning, Helene made pancakes, eggs, and bacon. It was a clear day, and John suggested a hike after breakfast. They drove to a nearby area where the trail began. It was over seven miles all the way up, but they planned to go about halfway, have the sandwiches they'd brought, and return. Mike and Robert led by about ten yards. By 1:00 p.m., they reached a spot they had heard about at the permit station.

There was a natural formation of smooth rocks clustered between some large pine trees.

"It smells like Christmas around here," said Darrell as they arranged themselves on the rocks for their picnic. Mike and Robert were a ways off, involved in an animated discussion. Then Mike was crouching low, his arms up, trying to prevent a mock shot from Robert, who at the last second pivoted and pulled around Mike to "score."

"They're having a ball," quipped John. Helene laughed.

"Mike took to Robert right away," she said as the boys came toward them.

"Did you work out some clever tactics?" John asked when Mike and Robert joined them to eat their sandwiches.

"Yes, Robert's a genius at it. You'd think he'd been playing basketball since he could walk," Mike said excitedly.

"I just love the game—the concept of it actually," said Robert shyly.

"Yeah, like war, right?" Mike added. "Like what you were saying last night."

"What's that, Robert?" said Helene.

"Something like a war—offensive or defensive, it's always one or the other during the game, although with each moment it shifts. As a player on the team, it's thrilling, like being on one side in a battle. You sense what the moves need to be, or before you turn around, the guys in the trench, they ain't talking French!"

"What does that mean?" asked Darrell.

"Just an expression for being beaten by the enemy," said Robert vaguely. John stopped chewing. Robert's rhyme was familiar to him in a way that all the years could not change. It had been coined by some infantrymen stationed in northern France during the First World War. It was their jargon for the fact they were helping the French fight the Germans. Sometimes, they'd say, "the boys in the trench, they'd better speak French" or something like that. After John returned from overseas at the close of the war, this type of expression had been popular for a short time. Then it had faded, and John had not heard it used since about 1921. John eyed the boy. Maybe his grandfather had fought in the war or some other relative. But Robert had used that line so naturally, so intimately that John had quivered with his own nostalgia. He had been there and heard it said just that way. He had said the phrase himself more than once.

John said nothing as they continued their outing. When they returned to the cabin, Helene asked Mike and Robert to go outside to get more firewood.

As they started out the door, Darrell said mysteriously, "Mike, you gotta help me finish that job now, remember?" Mike nodded and said he had to stay.

John rose, saying "I'll go with Robert—it's too close to dusk to go alone. We'll be back soon with a heap of wood."

They went downhill, past some other cabins, and then turned left onto the dirt road that led to a wooded area of about ten acres. They had a big flashlight, but that wasn't necessary yet. The sky was a medium gray except for a somber orange hue in the west.

"You just started at Madison High this year, right?" John asked.

"Yeah, my dad and I moved here from Ohio."

"Just the two of you?"

"My mother died when I was four."

"Oh, I'm sorry. What made you move here?"

"My father's company moved their headquarters here. He still has to travel a lot, but we're based here. I'm alone a good amount of the time, so I appreciate coming this weekend, thanks."

"You're very welcome, Robert. Tell me, besides your father, do you have grandparents or anyone?"

"No one here. Back in Ohio I have an aunt."

"That's all?"

"Yup. She's a nurse, lives by herself."

This information, or lack of it, nipped at John as they collected the wood. They walked back with Robert holding most of the wood and John guiding them with the flashlight.

"There was something you said earlier today, Robert, something about basketball being like a battle. You made an unusual comment—men in the trench was it?"

"The guys in the trench, they'd better speak French. That one?"

"Yes, that's kind of different. Where'd you pick it up, back in Ohio?"

"No, I heard it in a movie. I think it was *The Longest Day*—yeah, that one—and it was so catchy. I pick up stuff like that." He watched the road as he spoke. John knew the film; it was about the D-Day landings at Normandy in World War II, and there was no such phrase in it.

They reached the cabin and started the fire. After dinner, Darrell presented John and Helene with the anniversary present he had made for them. It was a plank of wood with many colorful rocks glued on it in the formation of "J&M." Mike had helped Darrell in the planning.

"We only had one disagreement," Mike said.

"Mike said it should be 'J&H,' but I wanted it to be 'J&M'—"John and Mom"—'cause I made it for you," Darrell said pointedly.

"It's beautiful," Helene said, giving Darrell a hug.

"Do you like it, John?"

"Oh, it's the best, son," John managed to answer, though distracted. His puzzlement was becoming an uncomfortable suspicion that he was trying to shake off, like a pesky kitten. Hours later, he was unable to sleep. Near 2:00 a.m., he went toward the kitchen to have some milk and cookies that Helene had baked. Robert was reading with his flashlight and looked up at John. Surprised, John whispered, "Couldn't sleep. Want to join me for a midnight snack?"

They sat on barstools at the counter that divided the kitchen and the living room and quietly ate. The smell and occasional crackle from the dying fire remained, echoes of the anniversary dinner. Mike snored rhythmically on the couch bed.

"You know about me," Robert said softly.

"Yes."

"What is it you think you know?"

"That you've been around at least since the turn of the century, fought in the First World War."

"You're the first person to perceive this about me in all this time."

"How much time, Robert?"

"Twenty years now. I was sixty-six years old in 1962, you know, getting on a bit. One morning, I woke up, and I was half that age!"

"Did you tell anyone?"

"Heck no. Thought I was going nuts. I just withdrew all my savings and left town."

"What about your family?"

"Didn't have anyone left really. Never got married. Took me quite a while to get adjusted—especially to getting younger."

"Younger?" John asked, realizing as he did that Robert was a teenager now, not a man in his thirties.

"Yes, I'm fifteen now, going for fourteen at some point." John gasped. Robert glanced at Mike, still snoring audibly. Then he looked at John.

"What's wrong? Too hard to believe?" But John couldn't answer. His neck felt paralyzed. "It's true, all right," Robert went on, savoring finally telling someone. "Actually, it's like going the other way—not much to do about it. I'll probably end up infantile instead of senile."

"I don't want to get younger," said John, trembling.

"You don't have to worry about—" Robert stopped short and gaped at John. "You! That's how you knew. Oh my God! You were older too!"

"I was eighty-seven a few years ago. Now I'm thirty-six or younger. I won't go through this. How can I? Helene can't be married to a teenager." A light went on in the hall, and Helene walked sleepily toward them.

"It's almost 3:00 a.m. What's all the noise about anyway?"

"Sorry, Mrs. Kettering," said Robert.

"Just talking sports, honey. Got a little carried away," John said, trying to smile. Helene took some cookies and returned to the bedroom.

John went to the window and stared out. Only a few stars beckoned. He lowered his head and tried to rub away tears that could solve nothing. Robert moved quickly to him, putting his hand on John's shoulder.

"Look, you may not be like me. It's such a fluke that we even met. Maybe you're going to age again. Even if you do get younger, you and Helene have time to work on that. Does she know anything?"

"No, and I hadn't planned to tell her."

"Well, plans can change. Give it some time and have faith."

"Faith in what?" asked John bitterly.

"In the way things are meant to be."

John slid into bed next to Helene and lay on his back thinking. It seemed like too big a secret to keep from her. Would she think he was mad if he told her the truth?

He decided to wait. Maybe it would be different for him. He hoped to God he would age.

◆ ◆ ◆

Five years passed. Mike was off at college, and Darrell had started high school. John had never seen Robert again since he had moved away after Mike's sophomore year. John knew he was getting younger. Their friends often commented on how well marriage had agreed with him, and people he worked with teased him about being a health nut. They wanted to know what kind of routine he followed. So far, he'd been able to modestly get around their remarks, but he couldn't indefinitely. He looked so good that women in their twenties showed interest in him. Once at a neighborhood cocktail party, a young lady had said to John bluntly, "You cute guys into older women fascinate me. What's the attraction?"

John felt sure that at least Helene hadn't noticed as yet. But then one evening when they were alone in the living room after dinner, Helene said, "John, there's something I've wanted to talk with you about for a while."

"What is it, honey? What did I forget to do?"

"Nothing like that." She paused and studied his face in a way he'd never experienced.

"John, I think there's something you're not telling me. I've thought it for a long time. I think something's changing between us because of it."

"Helene, I don't know what you think is going on, but I'm not involved with anyone—if that's what you—"

"I did think that at first," she said, cutting him off. "Another probably younger woman. But then I realized something."

"What?"

"That I always knew where you were. Besides, I just don't think you would be unfaithful to me. They say most men are, but I decided to trust you." She didn't seem finished. "But am I right? Is there something?" John looked at Helene, whom he loved so dearly. How would she take what he was about to tell her?

The sun warmed the big park. Spring had finally come. The wide paths stretched across the grassy slopes. Children ran with kites, followed by barking dogs. On one bench sat two elderly ladies. One knitted while she talked with the other. She had silver hair that waved under a thin net. Her friend was stocky, and her puffy legs didn't touch the ground. Not far from them, a small boy played with his ball. He moved closer and closer to them.

"Careful, Johnny, don't bounce that ball onto my knitting."

"Oh, I won't," he said playfully, and still too close. "Don't you trust me?"

She grinned and put her wool and knitting needles into a bag. "Actually, it's time to go. Goodbye, Ruth. Maybe we'll see you tomorrow."

"That would be nice. Goodbye, Helene. So long, Johnny."

Part IV

Essay (1998–2017)

Coming of Age

On October 5, 1997, I turned fifty. I'd spent the previous year thinking about the approaching half-century marker and noticing that I was not dreading it the way so many do. I was kind of excited about it. I felt like a war-wearied veteran and proud of it. I'd earned every second of every minute it had taken to hit the big five-oh! I'd lived decades evolving into the person I was and would continue to do so. I felt the mileage traveled, the energies spent, the images blown, and the identities developed, experienced and then shed like a reptile's skin.

I was raised in the 1950s in New York City, believing that girls grow up and marry Prince Charming–type men who take care of them. Of course, you had to be pretty, interesting, and not too pushy. Attracting men was a skill I learned early by watching my divorced mother date. Utmost attention was paid to hair, makeup, and figure-revealing clothes. When, at eleven, I needed my first bra, I was mortified. My mother happily said, "In just a few years, you will be so glad you fill this out, darling." She sort of identified with the Gabor sisters, Zsa Zsa and Eva, because her father was Hungarian. Men couldn't resist the Gabors and, for the most part, my mother. The role of coquettish female was one I perfected watching her answer the door when her date for the evening arrived. There were lots of subtle body postures, softened voice inflections, giggles, and shy looks. I also watched my grandmothers, Sara and Goldie. They were devoted to my grandfathers and took pride in giving me the kind of orientation I would need to fulfill my roles in life of wife and mother. I never thought about working. Work was for women who needed money, but since my family had plenty while I was with them and then a husband would take care of me, it wasn't something I had to do. I married at seventeen and was taken care of by my twenty-two-year-old husband, for whom I was accommodating and eager to please. I liked having him make all the big decisions. In 1970, at twenty-two, I gave birth to our daughter. Shortly after that, my husband decided that we should move from New York to Los Angeles for a job offer he'd received. The cross-country move and living adjustment was disruptive beyond repair, and eventually the marriage dissolved.

By the time my daughter was five, I finally entered the workplace, starting as a waitress in a deli in Beverly Hills. Being out in the world earning money was quite liberating. Unfortunately, I got fired! The cook had a crush on me, and when I turned down his invitation for a date, he took it real hard. After that, he'd throw my customers' orders at me while cursing, and the food would be done wrong. He'd make a sandwich on white instead of rye bread as ordered, and when I pointed that out he'd say, "Tough shit, bitch!"

Finally, the boss, a sturdy, silver-haired matron named Marge let me go. She said, "Joanne, you're a terrific waitress, but they're a dime a dozen, and a good cook is hard to replace. John's kind of strange, but he's been here seven years, and he said it's either him or you!" Today, I'd have one heck of a lawsuit for having been so treated, but it was 1975, and if I had legal recourse then, I wasn't aware of it. I left and got another waitress job but quit after one week of being surveilled by a Big Brother–type camera that probably followed me into the bathroom.

I decided I was done being a waitress and decided to try getting an office job.

My ex-husband was a television executive, and during our marriage he had brought his brother into the business as well. I spoke with both of them about needing a job, and my ex-brother-in-law knew of an opening as a secretary for two talent bookers on *The Tonight Show* with Johnny Carson. I interviewed with them and got the job, working at NBC in Burbank in 1975.

It was my first full-time, company-benefitted job and I was almost thirty. I worked hard and tried to be the best possible secretary, which wasn't that different from trying to be the best possible wife. My eagerness to please defined me. When, after two years, I was offered a six-month, freelance-talent-booking job, I took it, giving up my secure position and benefits because getting off a secretarial desk in 1977 was clearing a hurdle of Olympic high jump size!

I spent my thirties building a production career, raising my daughter, and continuing to try to find that elusive Prince Charming. Even though I wasn't a secretary, I still thought like one in my life. My job was to serve, to please, to garner approval so I could look in the mirror. People would tell me to "stop apologizing" for myself, my acts, my very thoughts, but I barely heard them. Wanting to be liked at all costs continued to drive my identity into my forties. Then something happened when I was forty-six. By then, I had moved back to New York to work, as I still do, as a television producer.

I was at the office having an argument with a production associate. She was angry at me for using a "condescending tone" toward her. I was desperately telling her, "It's not how I meant what I said" and repeating my exact words so she would understand and believe me. Her unmoved stare told me that we were at an impasse. She didn't buy what I was saying; she wasn't even listening. I, who had perfected finding any kind of crack, even in a cement wall, was facing an irrevocably slammed door. I retreated, feeling twisted by my failed efforts. She didn't like me, and no way I could try to be would get her to like me. A panic started overtaking my body, the shock that my identity was on the line. Trembling, I went to the ladies' room, whipped into a stall, and started to cry, feeling devastated. Then, a voice in my head said loudly, "So she doesn't like you—*so what?* You're still standing. You're still you. Not everyone has to like you!" These words became a mantra from that moment on. Their truth blindsided me. It was such a meaningful moment there in the ladies' room stall that when I unlocked the door and came out, I felt altered.

Letting go of having to please and be liked has meant being someone I'm still getting to know. I'm so much more relaxed, I almost fall off chairs. My jaw has been liberated from its frozen smile. I am not propelled to talk all the time because being quiet no longer means not being enough. Feeling comfortable with myself on the inside is easier than on the outside. Cosmetically, the fear of wrinkles, bags, and sags is perpetuated nonstop by every visible media outlet so that it is almost shameful to age.

I gristle at the mentality of our youth-obsessed culture, which views the word *old* as dirty, and certainly not hip or happening. I am "happening" much more at fifty than when I was in my twenties. This line of thinking enrages me, partly because I followed it for so long myself. It can shake the tree of my newfound confidence. I work hard not to let it. I say my age even as people around me in their thirties don't want to reveal theirs. I respect those older than myself and view them as sources of supreme wisdom. I want my twenty-seven-year-old daughter to have me as her reference for what fifty is all about.

On Aging

I don't want to be a woman who is afraid to look or be old. Being my age feels earned. Every second it took to be right here, right now was the time I needed, the time I was blessed to have. Time is the blessing we all need to be, and more time is a greater gift, so I am not negative about aging.

I don't want my self-love and self-worth to be contingent upon how I look. I don't want to be valued more for smooth skin than wrinkled. The fear of aging seems chronic in America. As evidenced by commercial ads, people seem obsessed with youth—how to have it and prolong it, as if aging were a plague. There's a lot that's great about being young. There are also benefits to becoming older, but they are not valued in our society. That's a shame for the young as well as the old. It's really true that if you knew then what you know now, you might have done life differently, but that is the whole point. It's what makes younger to older meaningful.

Another not-valued thing in our youth-obsessed arena is wisdom. It is gained by the dues-paying circumstances of living long enough to start to have some of it. Wisdom can occur in youth, but it is not the same as that which comes with age. You have to grow old for that component of wisdom. Again, it's the mileage logged. If we get to be old, it means we've added more hours, minutes, days, and so on into years. Layers of experiences, memories, and life data just keep accumulating. Think of what your layers amounted to at ten, at twenty, and so on. I'm in my sixties now. I can reflect on many decades of living through all kinds of events, both personal and historical. I am amazed at how uninterested young people are in what I (and the senior population in general) might have experienced or witnessed because I was living at the time. I understand that part of being young is thinking everything of any importance started today or maybe yesterday at most. When I was young, I certainly thought that. What surprises me is that as people age, so many of them don't value their ongoing journeys. They freak out about the "loss" of youth instead of celebrating the "gain" of middle age, then old age. The awareness of mortality that increases with age is, I'm sure, part of the equation. Maybe even the part that drives the obsession with youth. Young means not being old enough to die. Still, there is only getting older or not, at any stage of life, at any age.

On Retirement at One Year

On September 28, 2007, one year ago today, I retired, after almost twenty years, from my job as a producer and talent executive for *Live with Regis and Kelly*. I had spent thirty-two years working in television.

I love being retired and am incredibly grateful that I do not have to go to work when I wake up in the morning. I cannot wait to get up now. Each day is a gift to unwrap. It is a kaleidoscope of colors and shapes that change with each moment.

I don't have to even know how the day will unfold. I can switch gears as I go along during the day, starting with one plan and then changing it up as I please. I had a lot of pressure with the last job I did, which I had been doing for over nineteen years when I retired. I love having a much more unpressured existence. I did love my job when I was doing it and felt very blessed to have it. I just found that I was done doing that job, having to spend my time doing that each day when I so wanted to spend my time another way.

Having each day for myself is very fulfilling no matter what I do with it. Some days I rest, read, and stay in bed attire until the afternoon. I love going slow, not being in a rush and being without a destination or task. When I do have something I want or need to do, I go and enjoy whatever it is.

Before retiring, I did fear possibly getting bored or having too much time on my hands, but so far, it is the opposite. I find the day is done and I haven't gotten to some of the things I thought I would when I awoke! People who told me that after retiring they wondered when they'd had the time to work were right!

I also had concerns about my sense of identity. Having spent the past nineteen-plus years as a television producer on an extremely popular talk show, I had an impressive media identity that to many was most enviable. What would the loss of my title and position be like? The answer surprised me. I actually feel more of who I am, not less.

I will still always have the work identity as part of my history, but I have spent this past year being myself meaningfully and newly. In fact, I am on a journey of discovery at sixty years old. I have embraced being a grandmother and am so thankful I could free up my time to enjoy this role hands on.

I am learning how to use my new Mac computer, and learning anything is so very stimulating. I look forward to learning many other things that intrigue me. Far from being bored, I am more engaged with whatever interests me. I no longer have to keep track of the Everest of job-related voice mails, emails, printed materials, and video data that I was paid well to know when I worked.

On Retirement at Two Years

It is August of 2009, and I am one year and ten months into retirement from my television career. That's what I retired from—working in television production. I retired from nothing else. In fact, these past twenty-two months and counting have been the most joyful I have ever lived. Retirement for me was not the end of anything other than my job. It was the beginning of a new chapter in my life that I had been longing to start. So far, this period has been most fulfilling and meaningful for me.

My new chapter is about having time to be. My relationship with time is quite changed. I can go very slowly, do one thing at a time, or not "do" anything with my time. I enjoy and savor my time now. I am calm, not stressed, and not rushed, and I love it! I am inward more and find that satisfying.

I feel my worth and value as intrinsic to my existence and not attached to identifying labels. This feels wonderful and without contingencies.

I have time for what I want to do and who I want to be. Spending time with my daughter and granddaughter is deeply fulfilling, and I am abundantly grateful to be able to do so often and with no conflicts of scheduling.

I derive purpose and accomplishment from being. It is not about what I "do" that defines me; it's about what I am. I have never been more of who I am than now, and I am evolving as I write.

On Retirement at Three Years

I have just celebrated my third anniversary of retiring. As the third-anniversary date came and went, I thought about how satisfying this time has been.

I had been under daily pressure at work and had to operate at an extremely fast pace, multitasking, juggling, constantly shifting the gears of priorities without notice or warning and doing so sometimes in a split, gut-tightening second. I got quite good at this and became masterful at it as the years passed, but being really good at something does not mean one necessarily wants to keep doing it.

Being able to "be" is most meaningful for me. I knew what I needed, and I got it for myself. I didn't need another job, hobby, activity. I needed to stop, breath, be quiet, be. I needed that as desperately as others need to be going, doing. I think my first six decades were about going and doing. They got me here where I want to be. Each of us on this planet has our own individual life, made up of our own unique-to-us moments as they occur. No two sequences of moments are the same. My moments lead me to today, to this moment, writing these words. I am deeply grateful for this moment, for every prior moment—even the very hard, painful, difficult ones—and I embrace all moments to come.

I know that for me it was the absolute right decision to stop doing the job, and I am beyond thankful that financially I was finally able to do so. Many people would love to stop working but cannot for economic reasons. I utterly appreciated getting the paycheck when I needed it. I never took any of the work perks for granted, and I gave 100-plus percent until I left.

It was not easy to accomplish my retirement for a myriad of reasons, but it has been overwhelmingly worth every step taken to get here.

On Retirement at Ten Years

Today is the tenth anniversary of my leaving my job at *Live with Regis and Kelly*. September 28, 2007, was a Friday, one week before I would turn sixty. I spent my last day at the job saying my goodbyes, and then at 5:00 p.m., I walked out of WABC-TV and on to Columbus Ave, my arms holding flowers, and started my next chapter. It has been a wonderful decade.

Being a "granny nanny" to Eve, supporting my beloved Judy, and spending countless hours with them both since I left the job is an unlimited source of fulfillment that I have each day.

During these past ten years, I put together and self-published a collection of poetry I had been writing since I was thirteen years old. This project had been a dream of mine, but only after leaving the demands of the job I held was I able to finally gather fifty years' worth of material. Some poems were still only handwritten in notebooks.

The Back Dock and other poems was self-published in 2014.

As I write this, I am putting together a varied collection of my writing that I plan to self-publish.

I truly loved my career in TV and most especially the almost twenty years I spent on the staff of *Live*. To this day, I am close to so many of my former work buddies and love them dearly. I am grateful to have their friendship; it is present and ongoing.

Part V

New Poems (2016–20)

Humble Warrior

I am your humble warrior
With every breath I take.
I've never been alone.
Before I had words,
I had you,
Within and beyond,
One part of the whole,
Always, forever,
Synchronized.

Judy

I watched as she came out of me
After the forceps turned her.
I saw her face before I knew
She was a she.
I heard the very first sound she made,
A startled whimper,
Not a wail,
No outraged scream
For having been moved
From the womb.
I heard the doctor say,
"It's a girl,"
And I said,
"It's OK, Judy"
As she continued to softly cry.
She came out sweet,
Her nature as gentle
That birth day
As it has been since.

For Eve

You are beloved to me.
I hurt when you do.
I feel so helpless.
I do not know how to
Comfort or console you.
I treasure every way you feel,
Every thought you think,
Always.

I Am a Tree

I am a tree.
Trees don't know
What is happening
In our country.
Trees resist
Severe storms
And will be here
Long after democracy
Is not.

For Beethoven

You are right here.
You understand.
We are connected,
Essence felt with every note,
No years between.
This is our moment,
Every time I can hear
Your soul reaching mine,
Thank you.

Z

Tiny, curious person
Solving jigsaw puzzles
Beyond your years,
Building Lego people and places
You inhabit with them.
Your parents nearby,
Your dog next to you
As you play,
Propelled by imagination,
Unrushed by the world.

Abbott Road

I know the sound of robins,
In March I hear them sing.
Still cold with snow piles melting,
They're here to herald spring.
They scour the ground for worms
And stake their trees to nest,
And soon the eggs they lay
Will hatch with all the rest,
Which have been laid
By every kind of bird,
Whose vibrant songs
Can now be heard,
A choir in nature's
Cathedral of trees,
The air filled with their joy
And hopes and needs.

Christmas Poem

Most special day,
Longed for,
Looked forward to,
Songs in celebration,
Hearts fill with love,
Tress dressed and lit,
With decorations kept
All year in boxes
Labeled "Xmas,"
The warmest of days
Even though it's
December 25
And snow might fall.

To Matter

You have to matter to someone,
There's no other way to survive.
If you matter to just one person,
Then you will know
You're alive.
To matter to more than one other
Is a blessing for some but not all.
To matter to oneself, regardless,
Is the key that opens the wall.

Teen of the Sixties

I was a teenager in the 1960s;
I wanted love, not hate,
Peace, not war;
Laura Nyro's song
"Save the Country"
Said everything,
Written after John Kennedy,
Martin Luther King Jr., and
Robert Kennedy were
Assassinated.
King had a dream I believed
Could come true
When I was a teen in the sixties.
And here we all are in 2020.
I am a senior, a grandma.
I still believe in love, not hate,
Peace, not war.
I am Hammerstein's cockeyed optimist
Amid those who spew hate, who always will.

Here

There is the back dock.
There is Central Park.
I am there.
I am here.
I am.

Acknowledgments

I am deeply grateful for the unwavering support I have received from my daughter, Judy Hammett. She has read much of the material in this book and offered insightful, focused, and caring feedback.

Thank you to my dear friend and memoir teacher Edith Sobel for her valuable guidance.

Always in my corner, cheering me on to keep writing and reading anything I hand him with undivided attention is my husband, Alan Saltzman.